her unexpected hero

a Checkerberry Inn novel

KYRA JACOBS

Dear Kate,
Happy reading!
xoxo,
Kyra Jacobs

her unexpected hero

a Checkerberry Inn novel

KYRA JACOBS

This book is a work of fiction. Names, characters, places, and incidents are the product of the author's imagination or are used fictitiously. Any resemblance to actual events, locales, or persons, living or dead, is coincidental.

Copyright © 2017 by Kyra Jacobs. All rights reserved, including the right to reproduce, distribute, or transmit in any form or by any means. For information regarding subsidiary rights, please contact the Publisher.

Entangled Publishing, LLC
2614 South Timberline Road
Suite 109
Fort Collins, CO 80525
Visit our website at www.entangledpublishing.com.

Bliss is an imprint of Entangled Publishing, LLC. For more information on our titles, visit http://www.entangledpublishing.com/category/bliss

Edited by Alycia Tornetta
Cover design by Liz Pelletier
Cover art from iStock

Manufactured in the United States of America

First Edition July 2017

Bliss

To the dreamers.
May you never stop believing dreams can come true.

Chapter One

Madelyn Frye stepped from her car in the Checkerberry Inn's meager lot, mentally gearing up for the night ahead. It was work enough to keep the inn's guests full and happy; it was something else entirely to please her elderly employer's bridge club. Usually Wednesday nights in mid-October were low-key, her job as chef the proverbial piece of cake. But with Ruby Masterson's group of ornery blue-hairs poised to descend on the place, there was sure to be a raucous of some sort or another. Of course, if catering for the persnickety group kept her boss happy then Maddie would do her best. Ruby had taken a chance on her right after finishing her culinary arts schooling, and Maddie would forever be indebted.

And if the kindly innkeeper would stop with her daily onslaught of matchmaking attempts, well, that would pretty much make her day.

"She's got a new one lined up for you, Madds."

Maddie groaned. So much for that idea. She turned and shot a dark look at Ruby's grandson Miles, who was making his way toward her.

"This is your fault, you know," she said. "If you hadn't fallen off the playboy wagon, she'd still be bent on finding a match for you, not me."

"It happens to the best of us, I guess." He chuckled, scratching at the fur growing low on his cheeks. Maddie would have never pictured him with a beard, but she'd be lying if she said it didn't look good on him. Oh, who was she kidding? The Masterson boys had struck gold in the gene pool, both fit, trim, and good-looking—three traits her parents had failed to pass on to her. "Which, of course, means your time is coming."

"Goodie for me."

"Oh, stop it. Your Romeo is out there somewhere."

"All I can say is, it's a good thing I like Stephanie so much, or I'd be trying to break you two up just to get Ruby off my back."

"She just doesn't want to see you sitting alone at the gala next month, is all," he said. "You get a date lined up yet? Because that would kill two birds with one stone."

Maddie bit back a groan. If she was asked that question once more before Stephanie's November "Second Chance Prom" charity event, she might deck someone. Why was it such a big deal for her to have a date? Stupid dance, it'd probably be a total bore anyway.

"Did you pay the invoice for the hors d'oeuvres?" she countered. "Because if you didn't, Stephanie will kill you and there won't be need for—"

"Maddie, dear?" Ruby called from the inn's back door. "A word when you have a moment."

"Be right there, Ruby." Maddie offered her boss a placating smile and muttered to Miles, "What's that all about?"

"I told you. She's got another match in mind for you."

"Who?" *Please don't say Arnold Shoemaker. Please don't say Arnold Sh—*

"Arnold Shoemaker." Miles winked. "And you know he's

quite the eligible bachelor."

"He's also nearly twice my age, has gaps in his smile wider than the Grand Canyon, and walks his pet goat around town on a leash."

Miles laughed. "Nothing a good set of dentures couldn't fix."

Maddie threw him one last scowl and headed inside. Apparently the matchmaking gene ran in their family, too. That one, she could live without. Though, with this stupid event just over a month away, her time to rustle up a date was growing short.

If only she could get Cute Guy from the Laundromat to notice her. Talk about the perfect guy to silence all the Masterson teasing. Cute Guy was at least six foot two and solid muscle from head to toe. Sort of like Brent, Ruby's other grandson, now that Maddie thought about it. But with brown eyes instead of gray. And oh, that smile. It made parts of her flutter like they hadn't in years. She'd adjusted her laundry schedule to match his on the off chance he might be in a smiling mood—living across the street from the Quarter Clean-It did have its benefits.

Not that she was stalking him.

Much.

She pushed thoughts of laundry and dates aside as she made her way down the back hall and through the dining room. Bridge night first, get serious about finding a date later. Maybe she could hit Walgreens on the way home, snag the latest Cosmo, and see if there were any new tips for picking up men. It was that, or ask the other women on staff at the inn for advice. Anyone other than Ruby.

"Oh, Madelyn. There you are."

Speak of the devil. "Uh, hi, Ruby. You...wanted to see me about something?"

"I know you're very busy, dear, but I was talking to Mary

Robinson in town this morning and she mentioned that her neighbor, that nice Arnold Shoemaker, isn't seeing anyone at the moment."

At the moment? Maddie did a mental eye roll. If that guy had had a date in the last five years she'd be surprised. Was Ruby so desperate that she'd already started digging to the bottom of Mount Pleasant's singles barrel?

"Look, Ruby, I really appreciate all you're doing for me, but—"

And then, through the haze of irritation, emerged a brilliant plan...

Lie.

All she had to do was tell a little white lie. Then maybe without being called to the carpet on a daily basis, Maddie could work the nerve up to actually find a date to this ridiculous dance.

She forced a grin. "—well, you see, I've already got a date. For the gala."

The words came out stilted as her conscience caught up with her mouth, but darn it, enough was enough. Besides, one little white lie couldn't hurt, right? And when she showed up at the gala with a guy on her arm, well, Ruby would be none the wiser.

"Why, Madelyn, that's wonderful." Her boss stepped closer, waggling her brows. "Anyone I know?"

"Ruby, is there anyone within a hundred-mile radius you *don't* know?"

"Ah, I see. You want it to be a surprise." Ruby nodded and stepped back to wave her on. "All right, dear. I won't hold you up any longer."

"Thank you."

Maddie continued on, her shoulders sagging with relief. If she'd known the fib would be so well received, she would have done this weeks ago.

"Oh, and Madelyn?"

She paused to look back. "Yes?"

"I can't wait to meet him."

Her boss's smile took on Cheshire cat proportions. Maddie nodded and continued on to the kitchen. *Neither can I.*

She made her way around the high-top bar that separated the dining tables from the kitchen's swinging double doors and was surprised to see her kitchen help already on dish-washing duty. Usually it was ten after four before Sarah moseyed in, which meant something was up. The ginger college sophomore had been gung-ho when she'd started working for them this summer, but the more business picked up, the less energized Sarah had become—which drove Maddie nuts. She had no tolerance for slackers, especially not in her kitchen.

"Hey, Sarah," she said, setting her things down and grabbing a clean apron. "How's it going?"

"Awful."

No head turn, no eye contact, and she was dressed all in black. Oh yeah, something was definitely up. Super—like Maddie didn't have enough drama to worry about with the bridge club event tonight.

"Sorry to hear that. Anything I can do to help?"

"Nope."

Okay then...

"Well, if you think of anything, just let me know, okay?"

Stone cold silence, broken only by the stirring of water as Sarah washed a mixing bowl about as slowly as humanly possible. Maddie bit back a curse, hoping the co-ed's pace would pick up as the night went on. Tonight was not the night for sloths and pity parties. Maybe a quick reminder would help get her butt in gear...

"So, you know we've got Ruby's bridge club to feed tonight on top of the usual group of guests." Maddie reached into the refrigerator near her and began retrieving trays of pre-made calzones. "Thankfully, prep time was half what I thought it would be. More dishes to start the evening, but less throughout your shift. That's a good thing, right?"

A cry, much like what could only be described as a turkey being strangled, rang out from across the room. Maddie turned to see Sarah raise a hand to cover her mouth as she stared down at her cell phone.

Twenty bucks says it's boy trouble again...

Stifling a sigh, Maddie stepped around the center island to check on the girl.

"Sarah, honey? Is everything all right?"

"All right? How can it be all right? He left me for that hater in Chem 201." A sob bubbled from the girl's quivering lips. "How could he *do* this to me? My life is *over!*"

Maddie offered her best—and most patient—motherly pat on the shoulder. "No, sweetie. Trust me, I promise that it's not. You just need to think of men as more of...accessories than staples. Remember, we've got fifty hungry ladies due to arrive—"

"Accessories?" Sarah's waterworks kicked up a notch. "But he was my everything!"

"I know, honey. But you'll be fine, really. It might take a day or two—" The sobbing grew louder, and Maddie cringed. "But you know what? If you just dig into those dishes and focus on your work, you'll forget all about Mark."

"Matt."

"Right, Matt."

Matt, Schmatt. This girl had been through three boyfriends since she'd started, which was less than four months ago. With each breakup, the drama levels had increased, but so far Maddie had always been able to talk Sarah back from the ledge. *This is just another hiccup. Nothing a little tough love can't cure.*

She reached around a sobbing Sarah to grab a freshly washed bowl and began drying it. "Why, another hour and you won't—"

"In another hour, he'll be with her." Her eyes widened, then narrowed. "Unless I get to him first."

Sarah ripped off her apron and sidestepped Maddie, angling for the corner where they stowed their purses.

Oh no. "W-what are you doing?"

Sarah didn't answer. Instead, she came back into view with said purse in hand and then paused to compose a text message, her fingers flying. Maddie bit back a growl.

"Sarah, honey, I need you. Clearly way more than Mark does."

The college co-ed threw her an exasperated look. "Matt!"

"Right, right. Please, just finish your shift. I'll let you leave early, okay? By then things between you two will have calmed down and everything will be fine."

"Oh, they'll be fine, all right. Because I'm not gonna sit around and let Hannah sink her claws into *my man*."

She brushed past and stormed toward the kitchen's rarely used side exit. Maddie watched her go, frozen in disbelief. Was Sarah actually walking off the job? *Now?*

"Wait! What about our dinner party?"

Sarah spun, arms flailing. "Dinner party? This is my *life* we're talking about!"

She'd been seeing the guy for a few weeks tops and suddenly he was her whole life? Maddie bit back an explicative-laced lecture on priorities and self-worth. "And this is *my* kitchen you're trying to throw a wrench into. Hear me, Sarah—you walk out that door and you're fired."

"Whatever."

Sarah slammed through the side exit and hurried off without another look back. Maddie followed her outside, contemplating chasing after her. But running had never been her strong suit, nor had tackling anybody. All she could do was stand there and gawk as the drama queen climbed into her car and then raced past, not batting an eye.

That's when the panic began to settle in.

There were fifty women due to arrive in less than an hour. Maddie had a kitchen full of half-prepped food, no dishwasher, and no backup help.

I'm so screwed.

She put a hand to her forehead and silently prayed for a miracle. Instead of the clouds parting, though, the wind kicked up. A nip of cold sent shivers down her spine, the first hint of what this winter had in store for them.

Maddie looked to the sky with a scowl. *How's that supposed to help me?*

Her answer came in the sound of tires on the main gravel road. Had Sarah had a change of heart after all? Maddie squinted in that direction, then gave herself a mental slap for giving the girl anywhere near that much credit. It was just a pickup truck, probably one of the locals.

But as she turned to head back inside, the truck turned onto the Checkerberry's long lane. As it drew closer, she realized it was the delivery truck from Granville's Hardware Store. Usually, she wouldn't have given it a second glance; today, it was like watching the Holy Grail be hand delivered. Because in that truck was likely old Tom's grandson, Cole, who'd been helping his grandfather ever since coming to town a few months back. He was healthy, able-bodied, and, if she'd overheard his grandfather's conversation correctly after church last weekend, looking to pick up some extra work.

Could she be so lucky?

Sure enough, Maddie spied a sunglasses-wearing Cole behind the wheel as the truck passed by, heading toward the barn to meet up with their resident groundskeeper. Between his stylishly shaggy dark blond waves and the scruff he sported along his chin and jawline, he definitely had the bad boy look going today. And though the thought of being trapped in a small space with someone that ridiculously gorgeous all evening made her a bit uneasy, beggars couldn't exactly be choosers. Not if she wanted to keep the blue-hairs happy tonight.

Besides, guys who looked like him never gave girls like her a second glance. And really, that was more than all right with her. Who had time for silly relationships when she had an inn full of people to feed? At least she did, so long as she didn't absolutely blow it tonight.

With a sigh she hurried after the truck, scrambling to think of what to say and praying he'd say yes.

...

Cole Granville eased past the Checkerberry's main building, radio low and mind spinning. Finally, a chance to put down anchor, to grow some roots had come up. He'd never thought the little shop two blocks from his grandfather's place would become available so soon. It was the perfect location for setting up his guitar lessons and repair studio, and today a For Rent sign had appeared in its front window. The problem was he needed to come up with money for the deposit and first month's rent by Friday.

He had about half that in the bank after scrimping and saving all summer long, doing any odd jobs he could find. Too bad half saved was still half short. No way would they let a virtual stranger sign a lease like that, even with his family connections.

Once he had a decent slate of weekly lessons, though, rent money would be no issue. Heck, he already had at least three kids from the nearby college on standby. Unfortunately, without a shop, his student roster was hard to build. Without a roster, his shop would be hard to support.

Talk about a case of chicken and the egg. If he weren't stuck working ad hoc odd jobs, things would be so much easier. But anything more and he knew it'd be a struggle to keep his employers in the dark about his past.

The past he'd walked away from in Texas this spring and hoped like heck to leave there.

Cole angled for the inn's old red barn, pulled to a stop beside a waiting Brent Masterson, the inn's groundskeeper, and climbed out of the truck to help unload the supplies he was delivering. Maybe he could swing by the Griffins on the way back into town, see if they had any more firewood needing chopped. Or the Schmuckers. It was still harvest season, right?

"Evening." Brent reached to unlatch the tailgate. "Thanks for running these out here. I knew I should have grabbed a few extra two-by—"

"Hey! You!"

Cole froze, his heart racing. The last time he'd heard those words, they were followed by "Stop! Police!" Resisting the urge to run, he turned toward the voice and stared. The Checkerberry's spitfire of a chef was running toward them, apron flapping in the wind.

"Uh-oh," said Brent. "What'd you do to make Maddie leave the kitchen at this hour?"

"No idea, I haven't seen her since church on Sunday. Maybe she's yelling at you?"

Brent chuckled. "Looks like we're about to find out."

She came to a stop a few feet back, her peaches and cream complexion flushed from exertion. "Hey, hi. Cole, right?"

The men exchanged a glance. Brent offered him a victorious smirk.

"Yes, ma'am. What can I do you for?"

"Ma'am? Good grief, I'm not ninety. Even if I do feel that way sometimes. It's Maddie. Just Maddie."

She put a hand to her chest. Cole's gaze followed the movement but he did his best not to let it linger there. He'd admired her curves from a distance many times, but never this up close. Today, her top was unbuttoned farther than it usually was on Sundays…

She cleared her throat and brought the hand down to plant on her hip. "You still looking for work?"

Cole stared at her, momentarily dumbstruck.

"Work." She waved a hand in front of his face. "Are you still looking for work?"

He blinked, trying to clear the fog of surprise from his mind. "Yes, ma'am—I mean, Maddie. Did you need help moving something? Or lifting?"

"No. More like washing dishes. You got two working hands and arms?"

"Yes, 'um."

"Then you'll do. Please tell me this was your last run of the day."

"It is." More like his only run of the day. Probably wasn't even necessary, but Old Tom hated to see him sit around bored on the days he filled in at Granville's Hardware. Not that he'd ever complain—those days were what graciously supplied the roof over his head until Cole got on his feet financially.

"Perfect. You finish with Brent, I'll call your grandfather." She hurried back toward the inn, leaving the men to themselves once more.

"Come on," said Brent with a grin. "I'll help you unload so you can get to our queen bee."

Cole smirked. "Thanks."

"I hope you didn't have any plans tonight. Big gathering up there, lots of old biddies. They stay longer than you'd expect."

"Nah, no plans." Cole looked back toward the inn, seeing it for the first time as a possible ticket to success. Who knew? If washing dishes paid a decent wage, maybe *he'd* find a way to stay longer than expected. And a cash advance.

In fact, his dream studio was counting on it…

Chapter Two

Maddie hung up with one surprised but approving Tom Granville, then set out to find Cole an apron before her nerves got the best of her. Because now, in the pre-chaos quiet, it was all starting to sink in.

Her and Cole Granville. Working together. All evening long.

She'd always found him cute in a country star wannabe kind of way. Between the frayed-bottom jeans, always worn in all the right places, the cowboy boots, and the wavy, nearly shoulder-length dark blond hair, he'd fit in on any Nashville stage. His bright blue eyes too often claimed her gaze, which would then inevitably shift to his lips. Because, oh, did she love the velvety voice that poured from them.

Lord almighty, the man could sing.

But singing and looking like a celebrity weren't what she needed from him right now. There were dishes to be washed and her sanity to be saved. Nothing more, nothing less.

A rap sounded at the kitchen's side door, one that few guests noticed as they passed it on their drive to and from the parking lot. Maddie hurried to let Cole in, fussing with the ties on a plain black apron swiped from their reserves. She shoved the door open with her hip, still focused on the blasted knot in one tie.

"Come on in. I've got an apron for you, keep ya—" She looked up as he brushed by, the scent of his musky aftershave momentarily scattering her thoughts. "Dry."

"'Preciate it."

He began stripping out of the blue-gray flannel he'd been wearing, a fitted white tee coming into view underneath. And darn if she wasn't suddenly tempted not to give him the apron…because a shirt like that all wet would show off the washboard stomach she suspected he was hiding underneath.

Oh my gosh, Maddie. Stop it. Stop. It!

She thrust the apron at him and looked away, mortified. Having Sarah in the kitchen had never messed with her libido. But having someone as delicious as Cole in here, only an arm's length or two away all night, might prove to be a little more…distracting.

Hmm, yet another reason she needed to hurry up and ask out Cute Guy. Clearly, she was in need of more attention from the opposite sex than she'd realized. Though, she'd never admit it around here—the Mastersons would jump all over that. Probably never let her live it down, either, since she was the resident bah-humbugger when it came to dating.

Only because her own track record had been so abysmal.

She started for the refrigerator, eager to put some space between her and that alluring scent of his. And view. And voice.

"So, uh, there's the sink." She waved in its general direction. "And the dirty dishes. Wash, dry, stack. Don't worry about putting things away—most nights I'm dirtying the same bowls several times. Over here is where we store the towels. Use as many as you need, we have a washer and dryer in the back corner. I'll start a load of wash before I go."

Maddie turned to make sure he was paying attention, as he'd remained silent as a church mouse. Sure enough, his gaze was focused on her, the apron now in place and tied back to front around his waist. And darn if he still didn't look good enough to eat.

"Any questions?"

"No, ma'am."

"Ugh. I'll break you of that habit soon enough." Cackling sounded from nearby, reminding her that time was short. Thanks to Sarah, she'd be scrambling all night. "You keep busy and stay out of my way and we'll get along just fine. Got it?"

He tucked some loose strands of hair behind his ear and grinned. "Got it."

"Oh! Your hair—we've got to do something about that." She looked around for something to hold it back. A hair net, a rubber band. Good gravy, she couldn't have one of Ruby's friends find a hair in their food!

"Will this do?"

Cole tugged a rolled-up ball cap from his back pocket and gave it a shake, then smoothed it down over his hair, backward. In an instant, he went from kitchen help she'd be struggling not to stare at all night, to man who was sure to star in a future fantasy. Because Cole Granville was far too sexy to be in her kitchen. Funny thing was, he didn't seem to notice.

Which to Maddie was the sexiest part about him.

He stared at her expectantly now, waiting for an answer. "Oh. Yeah. Sure." She brushed past him and began re-stacking a pile of dirty dishes at the sink. "What's the 'T' for?"

"Texas Rangers. Grew up a fan."

"Texas, huh? Explains the cowboy boots you're usually in. On Sundays. Not that I..." *Grr*, could she dig this hole any deeper? She didn't dare look at him, just shuffled over to the island kitchen and waved for him to take his place at the sink. "Well, anyway, don't let Miles see you in that, the crazy Yankees fan. He'll think you've sided with Brent and the Tigers."

Cole chuckled. "I doubt he'll get the two confused, but thanks for the heads-up."

Good lord, even his chuckle is silky smooth.

One shift. All she had to do was make it through one shift with him here. Tomorrow, she'd ask Miles to find her a suitable replacement for Sarah, someone a lot less fun to look at. Maddie closed her eyes, drew in a deep breath, and got her head back in the game. She had a room full of her boss's friends expecting perfection.

Because while Maddie absolutely stank at the dating thing, perfection in the kitchen she could do.

...

Cole toweled off the last mixing spoon and set it in the drying rack, surprised at his level of exhaustion. Who would have thought washing dishes could be so tiring? He'd worked his tail off, trying to impress his temporary boss. Because if his dream studio was to become a reality, he needed this job to last more than one night.

He twisted slowly from side to side, then bent to reach for the floor, trying to knock loose the kink that'd settled into his back the last half an hour or so. Seems he wasn't used to standing so long in one place. Heck, he wasn't used to being in one place so long period. Upside down, he chanced a brief look at Maddie, who'd finally slowed from breakneck speed to something more along the lines of a leisurely jog. He'd never seen anyone so focused on their work, her brows frequently drawn low in concentration. When she'd been pleased with something, she'd start to hum a little tune—

nothing recognizable, as she seemed to be rather tone deaf, but a happy humming all the same. If something didn't go her way, expletives followed and not always quietly. It was those times he found it wise to keep his eyes on the dishes, rather than the chef.

Though, the chef sure was fun to admire. She seemed completely unaware of how adorable she looked smattered with flour, her pinned-back hair loosening with every brush and nudge she gave it with her forearm or the back of her hand. Back home, the boys would have scooped a woman like her up in no time. Sexy *and* she could cook? It was every homeboy's dream.

"Sore?"

Cole bolted upright and felt the room swim around him. He reached for the nearest counter to steady himself, light-headed from the sudden movement. "Nah," he said through gritted teeth. "I'm good."

"You're too skinny is what you are. Here." Maddie slid a plate full of ham and potatoes toward him. "My way of apologizing for working you through dinner. I tend to get pretty wrapped up in my work."

He stared down at the meal, a lump forming in his throat. Simple acts of kindness weren't something he'd experienced much over the years. "Thanks."

"Don't thank me, Skinny, just eat. Before some breeze kicks up and knocks you over like a bean pole scarecrow."

He dug in, too hungry to argue the point that he was not too skinny, or that he'd never been knocked over by Mother Nature. Though, eating meals like this? Now that was a rarity. He might never have tasted anything so delicious in his life.

"You like?"

Cole nodded, unwilling to stop shoveling long enough to speak. Man, he could get used to eating like this. Ham that didn't require a steak knife to cut? Creamy, cheesy potatoes that melted in his mouth? It'd be worth the wait every time. He set the fork down and swiped the edge of his apron across his mouth.

"I never knew ham could taste so good."

"Well, then you've never had my ham before."

She went back to her work, which appeared to be prepping a future meal. But he didn't want her to go back to work, not when he was still dying for some reassurance that he'd get to come back tomorrow. "So, uh, is this your own recipe then?" He cringed. *Man, could you sound any lamer?*

"Yep."

"Seriously, it's delicious. What's in it?"

She shot him a wary look. "Why do you want to know?"

"Just curious." He shrugged. "And trying to make small talk now that you're not, you know, cussing out the beets anymore."

"I cuss out a lot of things," she grumbled, a flush creeping up her cheeks. "Would have cussed at you if you'd gotten in my way one more time."

"One more time?" Cole grimaced. He'd tried so hard to do everything right. The first hint of doubt cast its shadow over his future at the inn.

"Yeah, well, Sarah and I had our timing worked out. If I was in the oven, she was drying dishes to leave me more room. If I was chopping vegetables, she was over there putting glasses away."

"You told me not to put anything away."

"Because I didn't want you dropping anything."

"Oh." She didn't trust him. He'd remedy that soon enough. "Well, you shouldn't worry about that. I've got unusually steady hands."

Maddie looked up with one brow arched. "Unusually steady?"

"Yep." He raised his hands and wiggled his fingers. "Years

of practice."

"And I'm sure those hands are far too expensive for my measly budget, so you might as well save your energy."

Crap. That wasn't the direction he was trying to steer her. The resolved look on her face suggested steering might not be an option with Maddie.

"Tough to say, as I have no idea what wage you're offering."

"Two bucks over minimum wage is what Sarah was making. Which reminds me—if you swing by tomorrow before the lunch rush, I'll make sure Miles pays you for tonight."

Two over? He wouldn't be raking in the dough, but it might help tide him over until he filled his student roster. Heck, he'd take anything he could right now…but that didn't mean he wouldn't try for more.

"You give me five over and I'll come back as many nights as you need."

"Five over? Are you nuts?"

Nope, just itching for my own run at the American dream. "Four over, that's my final offer. Unless, that is, you'd like to work solo for a week or more while you run an ad in the paper?"

She froze in mid-chop and met his gaze. "A week or more?"

Ah-ha—she did need help as badly as he'd hoped. Cole worked to keep his features cool, calm, and collected. "Sure. The paper'll take a few days to list anything. Applicants will have to send in their resumes. That is, unless you have an online application."

"Well, no…"

"See? So there's a few more days. And then there's interviewing, background checks…"

Maddie cursed and looked to the ceiling. Cole watched her stew in silence, hoping he'd painted a bleak enough picture for her.

"Heck for that price, you ought to be working two jobs for me." She set her knife down—which was more than fine with him—and gave him a wary look. "How are you with relationships?"

"Come again?"

"Relationships. And dating. If I'm going to pay you that much, you're gonna earn it."

"Oh. Uh…" Okay, this was so not where he thought the conversation would head. Surely she wouldn't want to get mixed up with someone like him. Someone with a history lurking in the shadows, ready to spring out and bite him in the butt. "You know, I'm flattered and all, but—"

"Not date *me*, for me." She shook her head, hands on the counter for support. "Here's the deal. There's a charity gala coming up and—"

"Gala?"

"Party, Cole. A fancy party. And I don't have a date lined up for it yet, even though Ruby thinks I do and if you tell her I lied I will hunt you down and—" She pinched the bridge of her nose. "Just…don't tell. Anyway, there is a guy I've been thinking of asking. I just…need a little guidance on how to actually do it."

"I see." Cole nodded, mentally breathing a sigh of relief while ignoring his stinging ego. But it made sense—a woman like Maddie would never go for a mess-up like him. He pushed that aside and tried to focus on the positives, like how her predicament gave him more leverage.

Leverage he planned to take advantage of. "Well, relationship coaching isn't something I've done on a professional level before, but yeah, I could definitely give you some pointers on what might turn a guy's eye, win them over."

"Really?"

"Sure. I'm a guy—kinda comes with the territory."

Her gaze narrowed. "Look, if you're going to make light of it just forget I asked."

"No, no, no—not making light, just being honest. Us guys? We're not so complicated."

"Uh-huh." She studied him for a long moment. "So if I can somehow pull off the request of the year from our finance guy, you'll wash dishes and help me get this date for the gala?"

"Absolutely. In fact, I'll do you one better. You give me two hundred cash by the end of the week, and I'll work for three dollars an hour over minimum instead of four."

"By the end of the week?" She barked a laugh. "Are you high?"

"Nope, just need some fast cash. And it's a win-win for us both. I did all right in here tonight, didn't I?"

She frowned, her gaze on the floor while her gears were clearly turning. Cole felt sweat bead at his hairline. If she didn't come through with the cash, he'd have to hit the streets tomorrow and hope for the best. He couldn't ask his grandfather for it—he already felt like a big enough burden as it was.

Maddie straightened, looking anything but pleased. "I've got some thinking to do. Come back tomorrow and we'll see."

"But—"

"Be here by four tomorrow, do as good a job as you did tonight, and I'll think about it. That's my final offer."

Darn it, what was there to think about? Either she needed the help or she didn't.

Then again, Maddie was the inn's chef, not its banker. Maybe she needed time to round up the money. Cole ran a hand over the back of his neck. He hated gambling on his future like this, but Maddie didn't strike him as a cheat.

He prayed this time he'd be right.

"Yes, ma'am," he said, stripping out of his apron. "But if that money's not in my hands by Friday at noon, I'll have no choice but to be moving on."

Chapter Three

Maddie climbed the steps to her apartment, wrestled the door open with what energy she had left, then closed and locked it behind her. What a day. While she was used to frequent surprises working where she did—especially from feisty innkeeper Ruby Masterson—today had been nuts. Like, *nuts* nuts. That harmless fib to Ruby must have ticked off the relationship gods or something because the rest of the day had gone downhill after that.

Lucky her.

"Hey, Fido, I'm home."

Her goldfish perked up as Maddie flipped on the kitchen lights, drifting to the water's surface in anticipation of his late evening meal. She shook a few flakes into his bowl, watched him inhale them in his usual nom-nom-nom style, then turned and grabbed a glass from the cupboard. There was a new box of Chablis in the refrigerator calling her name tonight. Working at the Checkerberry might be physically exhausting, but her mind had a habit of kicking into high gear after the dinner rush, consumed by ideas for the next meal, or how to make the last one better. Ideas, ideas, ideas. And now Cole.

Thank goodness for wine, otherwise known as Maddie's cure for overthinking. Half a glass was all she'd need to dull the hum and allow her to relax.

She reached into the fridge, unable to ignore Stephanie's silver glitter covered gala invitation hanging from a magnetic clip on the freezer door. Why had she let both Miles and Ruby get under her skin earlier? Now she not only had to come up with a boyfriend in a matter of weeks, but convince him to attend this silly second-chance prom event, too.

Then there was the whole deal with Cole. A dating coach? Had that idea really come out of her mouth?

Maddie shook her head and pushed the wine box's stopper in. If she'd been smart, she would have just asked him to go to the gala and been done with it. But his good looks and close proximity had left her feeling intimidated, so she'd sidestepped the invite and asked for his help instead. Probably a good thing, since he clearly wasn't interested.

"I'm flattered and all, but..."

But. Of course there was a *but*. Like high school all over again.

She took her more-full-than-usual wineglass to the living room and sank down onto her couch with a sigh. No, it wasn't nearly as bad as high school. At least now she was free of braces and raging acne. Plus, growing her hair out in college definitely had her looking much less like a boy. But even with all those changes, she still wasn't confident in social settings. Growing up an only child hadn't helped her much with that. Neither did being raised by a grandmother who worked from before dawn to after dusk and who expected no less of her.

An expectation that seemed entirely normal and didn't bother her for many years.

Living in a small farming community in northern lower Michigan, it wasn't often Maddie saw other kids her age outside of school during their elementary years—most of them were expected to help with their own families' businesses. But as she and her classmates moved on to middle and high school, priorities changed. The farm kids were suddenly spending more time away from home, gearing up for sports scholarships and college, while Maddie was confined by absent parents, a tough economy, and an ailing grandmother. Sure, she'd envied the other kids from time to time. But she'd never blamed her grandmother or bemoaned their situation—she just accepted it and did the best with what she had. A good thing, since time with her Grandma Bea was coming to an end sooner than either of them would have liked.

She took a sip of wine and sank lower into her secondhand plaid fabric couch. So much had changed since high school. Since college, and the wool getting pulled over her eyes by Harrison. Since losing Grandma Bea.

But Ruby Masterson had brought her out of those dark days and back into the light. A little faith in her had gone a long way, and beneath Ruby's ever-encouraging gaze Maddie's chef skills had flourished. Not that she hadn't been good before, but now she had the confidence to go with it.

Confidence in the kitchen, that was. Everywhere else she still felt like an outcast. Now she had a Cute Guy to win over, her fragile ego to protect, and a kitchen to share with a man whose voice alone was enough to make her knees go weak, let alone the very sight of him.

Maddie took a good long drink and turned her gaze to the ceiling. "Could use a little help from you up there, Grandma. 'Cause I have no idea what kind of mess I'm about to get myself into."

...

Cole sat on a worn, three-legged chair in his room, guitar on one knee, eyes closed, and face turned to his window and the starry sky beyond, dreaming. The recent turn of events sure felt like a dream, anyway. A few more dollars in his wallet and a nod from Sheridan Realty, and the business he'd first envisioned while doing time might just become a reality.

His own guitar shop.

For as long as he could remember, life had been tough. The memories of his father had grown more and more faded as the years went by, but he held on to the knowledge Luke Granville had been a good man. Hardworking, dedicated to his family. The accident on I-27 north had been unpreventable, according to the people who know such things. Ice was rare in Lubbock, and Texans invincible. Or at least, the ones who insisted he make that last delivery by five o'clock rather than wait a few hours so the sun could melt the ice away must have thought all Texans were invincible. Cole's father and the pickup truck driver who T-boned his semi had unfortunately proven otherwise. That left Daisy Mae Granville with no husband, no income, and a little boy who asked day and night when Papa would be coming home.

Daisy Mae. Cole felt the muscles in his neck tighten—a natural reaction to thinking about his mother. In his younger days, he'd felt bad for her, losing so much so fast. She and Luke had married young and hit the road, thrill seekers looking for adventure. What they got was her pregnant the minute they stepped foot in Texas and Luke a trucking job to provide for his growing family. Often, Cole and his mom joined him on the road, her hating to be alone and Cole having no choice but to go along for the ride. But he adored his father, looked up to him, and never minded the long hours being stuck in that semi's cab.

Blue. It'd been blue with a white eagle hand-painted on each of its doors. In the eagles' talons were two yellow daisies—one for him and one for his mama, held safe from harm.

But the eagles hadn't protected them any more that fateful day than they'd protected his father. In fact, if Luke hadn't insisted they stay behind that day, all three would have perished. Lost without the man who'd always seemed bigger than life, Cole turned to music; his mama to alcohol. Together, they hit the road, looking to escape the pain of their past.

But finding work is tough for the uneducated, even tougher when they're drunk. Cole loved his mama and tried his best to help however he could. Odd jobs, doing work around whatever motel or rental place they were staying, cooking, cleaning—you name it, he was on it. And while his mother slept off whatever hangover she'd incurred, Cole woke with the sun, softly strumming tunes on his dime store guitar.

While he slowly healed, Daisy Mae had gotten deeper and deeper into her addictions, trading alcohol for something much more lethal: drugs. Cocaine eventually became her habit of choice, landing her in jail on charges of possession when Cole was thirteen. That was the summer he'd come to stay with his Grandpa Tom and Grandma Eileen—the most carefree summer of his life. Their chore list had been limited, the depths of their love unending.

He'd cried when they put him on the plane back to Texas, but put on a brave face for Daisy Mae. She'd looked healthy waiting for him at the airport, smiled and hugged him so tight he thought he'd break in two. He'd felt guilty for crying, for not wanting to come home, until he caught sight of the man she introduced as her boyfriend. The verbal abuse only took a few hours to begin. The physical, well, Cole got really good at disappearing when the fists started flying. His mother? Not so much. Each time Cole convinced her to leave and stay away from one brute, she'd turn around and find another who treated her just as poorly.

Apparently, that was the culture drug users were used to.

Cole, however, wanted nothing to do with it. At wits' end, he packed his mother and all their things into the beater car she still had of his father's the week before he turned eighteen. She'd argued with him, said it was wrong to run from their problems instead of face them like adults. But he hadn't listened, just drove as far as that tank of gas would take them. He lectured her the entire way about how it was time for her to get clean, to make something of herself. He wouldn't be around forever to watch out for her. At first she'd been sullen, bitter. But by the time they reached the town of Happy he felt like he'd finally gotten through to her. She was talking about going back to school, maybe finding work at a nursing home taking care of the elderly.

And as desperate as he was to see her succeed, he'd believed her. What a fool he'd been.

That same night he'd woken to find her gone. The motel's door was ajar, their car missing from the lot. Cole had assumed the worst, worried she'd been taken by the monster they'd just traveled all this way to escape. He'd grabbed his gun—protection his grandfather of all people had equipped him with—and headed into town, praying he'd find her in time.

The tightness in his neck increased as the rest of the memory played out. Finding Daisy Mae, strung out on whatever drug she must have had on her, dragging crates of alcohol out the back door of a shop she'd clearly broken into. Him begging her to abandon whatever crazy idea she had. To get clean, to start a new life.

The flashlights shining, the police shouting, someone finding his gun.

His mother, eyes glazed, shoulders slumped, and not saying a damned word in his defense.

Seven years had passed since that day. He'd done his time, completed probation, and was a free man in the eyes of the Texas legal system. But it was the eyes of everyone else he worried about. Eyes in a new town, eyes that wouldn't understand.

This guitar shop would go a long way toward easing his mind. To healing his wounds and helping him move beyond his past. To become part of a community for the first time in his life.

Cole drew in a deep breath, exhaled, and opened his eyes. Mount Pleasant was as good a place as any to put roots down. Better even, with his grandfather here, offering his unending emotional support. Though, it remained to be seen if Mount Pleasant would grow to accept him as easily as he'd grown to accept it.

He looked out his bedroom's small window to the Quarter Clean-It, the laundromat's old-fashioned neon orange sign bringing Maddie Frye to the forefront of his thoughts. Pink had tinted her pretty face as she'd admitted to needing help last night. *His* help. Of course he'd wanted to help her—he'd proven repeatedly over the years that he was a sucker for a damsel in distress. Too bad his mother had burned him one too many times playing that role. Now his help was going to come with a price tag.

Hopefully, he hadn't set the price too high.

Chapter Four

Maddie eased into the Checkerberry's kitchen the next morning at four thirty, savoring the blessed quiet. And stillness. Unlike last night, there was nothing in here to distract her or make her self-conscious. No worrying about whether or not her top gaped open too much when she bent to retrieve a dish from the oven or if her panty lines were too obvious through her thin black pants. The worries had left her unsettled, bothering her to no end. After all, the kitchen was her sanctuary, the place she felt most comfortable in. Where she was most in charge.

Last night, that confidence had been seriously tested by one Cole Granville.

Not because of anything he'd said or done, but by the simple fact that he was a member of the opposite sex. She hadn't dressed to spend the evening in the company of men, she'd dressed the way she always did: in clean, professional clothes that didn't impede her work in the kitchen. White button-down shirt with the sleeves rolled up, black slacks, comfortable black socks and shoes—definitely nothing to write home about.

Of course, Cole being too attractive for his own good only added to her ire. And though from what she could tell he'd kept his eyes on the sink and not on her, she still couldn't help but wonder if agreeing to let him stay on would be a mistake. Then again, if she could learn to ignore him it'd be to her advantage—he was twice as efficient as Sarah. Maybe even more than that. The man was a machine, washing dishes nearly as fast as Maddie could dirty them.

And did he really know anything about relationship coaching? Bah, she must have sounded completely pathetic. But the wild hair of an idea had slipped out before she had time to think about its ramifications, and there was no taking it back.

Which led to this morning's dilemma: how to get "Mr. Scrimp and Save" Miles—otherwise known as Ruby's second grandson and the inn's chief financial officer—to cough up two hundred bucks by Friday. And to increase wages for their kitchen help, which would be tough enough as it was. Lord knew she and Miles had already butted heads over increased expenditures far too often this year.

But Cole did do a great job last night. And she really needed help getting a date for the gala before the others found out about her fib and gave her grief for, oh, the rest of her life. What to do, what to do? With a sigh, she put her things away, pulled out a fresh apron, and flipped on her tunes. Maybe a few hours alone in the kitchen would give her time to come up with a plan.

There were no guest rooms above this portion of the inn, only an open seating area beside the main stairway's second floor landing. That meant not having to worry about making too much noise in the kitchen, or that anyone would hear her singing along with the radio. And though she loved having the space to herself, Maddie had never gotten used to the silence that came with working alone. Growing up, she'd had her grandmother there, chattering away in between tasks. She'd planned on Grandma Bea being around to help get her dream cafe off the ground after college. But life doesn't always go as planned, and Bea's heart attack a few years ago ended hers far too soon.

Maddie tugged a heavily scribbled upon index card free from her recipe box and gave it a quick once-over. Today's breakfast feature was to be "Cheddar Hashbrown Triple Treat Surprise," otherwise known as "pork overload." If the cheese and biscuits didn't fill their guests up, the sausage, ham, and bacon would. It was a fairly new recipe of hers, perfected just these past few months, but it had been a big hit with Ruby's guests so far. A good thing, as happy guests led to good reputations, and good reputations could someday land her in a bigger, more upscale kitchen with the budget for more than a single evening dishwasher. But that was down the road a ways. For now, she would count her blessings—Ruby had taken a chance on her, after all—enjoy her reign over the Checkerberry's modest accommodations, and keep doing the best she could.

Voices and footsteps sounded in the dining room about the time Maddie was sliding the first batch into the oven.

"Mmm, I smell bacon."

She looked up to spy Miles push past the swinging doors that separated the kitchen and dining room. Hot on his heels was Stephanie Fitzpatrick, Miles's girlfriend and perfect match. Steph also happened to be the only woman alive who'd been able to tame the former playboy, and she kept him in line quite well. Maddie had instantly liked her, for that if nothing else. This morning, both intruders to her kitchen were dressed in running gear and glistening with sweat. A quick glance at the clock found it to be after six.

"You came in here for a glass of water," Stephanie

said, giving Miles a light rap on his shoulder. "Not to get in Maddie's way."

"I won't." Miles ambled deeper into the room and angled for the glasses. With a wink, he swiped a strip of cooling bacon from a nearby tray. "But this bacon? Well, it was definitely in the way. So you're welcome, Madds."

Maddie jabbed her tongs in his direction. "You just remember that the next time you think about giving me grief over meat market invoices, buddy."

"Whatever. One strip of bacon won't blow our budget." He retrieved a glass and filled it at the sink. "A good thing, since business will be winding down for the season. Revenue's gonna start tapering off soon."

She cringed. "Uh, yeah. About that…"

Miles's gaze narrowed in mid-drink. Maddie drew in a calming breath and braced herself for the oncoming battle. Asking him for money was like ripping off the bandage of a perpetual sore spot.

"I need to raise the wage for my kitchen help. By three dollars an hour. And offer them a cash advance."

Miles slammed his glass down. "Are you nuts? We can't afford that!"

"Actually, I think we can. And before you have a coronary, just hear me out. I had to fire Sarah last night. She walked out on me an hour into her shift after getting a breakup text from boyfriend number forty-three of the year. Left me scrambling, and not for the first time. So I told her to either get back inside or not come back."

"Let me guess—her world was ending and she couldn't understand how you could be so cold and heartless." Stephanie smirked.

"Pretty much. Kids these days." Maddie shook her head. Bea would have swatted her butt good for being that irresponsible. "Anyway, about that time Granville's delivery truck came barreling up the drive. I knew Old Tom's grandson was looking for some extra work, so I tracked Cole down. Talked him in to covering for Sarah last night. And I'm telling you—this guy's amazing. You should have seen him in here—he was a monster with those dishes. Careful, thorough, quiet. Never complained once. Better yet, we finished half an hour earlier than usual. And that was his first night! If he gets faster with a little more experience, we'll end up paying him fewer hours than we would have paid Sarah. So the increase in salary will just…even out."

Miles grabbed his cell phone and started tapping numbers onto the screen. "If you can keep his hours down, maybe. But we can't go over what we were paying Sarah, Madds. We took a hit bringing her on—I'd hate to give up any more income than we already have." He looked up to meet her gaze. "You really think you need the extra help now that our season is winding down? Who knows how long we'll be able to support him. A few weeks, maybe? And the cash advance is a definite no go, unless you want to skip buying ingredients this week."

Dang it, why had he picked today to rattle off such bulletproof reasoning? The boost in business this season had been a much-needed surprise and allowed them to remain open longer than in the past. Unfortunately, no one knew when business would start to drop off, only that it would once the neighboring golf courses and tourist sites officially closed for the season. Maddie leaned back against the counter and crossed her arms.

"You still planning to keep the place open until the end of November?"

"Yeah, but that's nearly six weeks off," he said. "And I seriously doubt occupancy rates will be worth a darn after Halloween. Heck, we may not have enough revenue coming in after that to pay you, let alone an extra set of hands in here."

"Could you find someone else?" asked Stephanie.

"Another college kid who's not asking for as much, someone to fill in for a couple weeks?"

"It'll take too long to find anybody else. I need help now. And I'm telling you, Cole is our guy."

Stephanie ran one hand up and down her opposite arm. "I know you do, it's just… Well, I'm not sure he's really who you all want working here."

Maddie looked to Miles, who shook his head, clearly as clueless as she was. "What? Why not?"

"Look, I shouldn't say anything, so this doesn't leave this room. But you know how we're taking camp counselor applications for next spring's Fun In The Sun program, right? Well, Ruby asked me to see if there were any spots Cole might qualify for. Since I wasn't sure which program he might like best, I brought it up with him after he finished playing at church last weekend…"

Maddie frowned. "And?"

"And he was quick to tell me not to put his name in at FITS. Started acting almost paranoid at the thought."

"So?"

Stephanie and Miles exchanged a look. Maddie rolled her eyes.

"Look, I don't know what kind of telepathy you two lovebirds have going, but stop it. Maybe he's just not a fan of working with kids or something. You couldn't pay me to take a job like that."

Miles chuckled. "Ah, Madds. Always so brutally honest."

"Which is bad, why?"

He shook his head and walked over to stand beside Stephanie once more. "True, it's possible that we're making mountains out of mole hills. But—"

"Imagined mole hills…"

"Regardless," he said. "If you want to bring him on, he can only stay so long as our rooms stay filled. Otherwise, we're going to have to make cuts elsewhere. And don't think your budget is safe from the axe, either."

"But if Kayla's fall advertising campaign keeps guests coming, it won't be an issue, right?" she asked.

"That's a big if."

"Well, an if is better than a no. So...do I have your blessing on this?" She clasped her hands.

Miles studied her for a moment. "We'll give it a try. But if he messes up, he's gone. And Old Tom's grandson or not, if he's got skeletons in his closet that are keeping him from applying at the foundation, he's not someone I prefer to have on our payroll, either."

"Like I said, imagined mole hills. He's a Granville, for crying out loud. I don't think that family knows how to live anything but the straight and narrow." *At least they'd better not, not for what it's costing me.* "And he won't mess up. I won't let him."

"I'm sure you won't." Stephanie grinned and took Miles by the hand. "Come on, honey. Clock's ticking. We'll run out of time for showers."

He raised her hand and pressed a slow kiss to it, a wolfish grin on his face. "Wouldn't want that to happen."

Maddie started forward, shooing them toward the door. "Okay, out you two go before you make me gag or something. Hard enough not to puke every time Brent and Kayla walk into the room. Now I've got to endure the likes of you, too."

"You'd better work on containing that gag reflex before the gala, Madds," said Miles. "Because I'm expecting to see your date with his tongue down your throat at least once that night."

Maddie grimaced. And maybe did gag a little. "Ew. No PDA."

"Don't knock it 'til you've tried it." Stephanie pulled Miles close, her gaze locked with his, and pressed a long, slow kiss to his lips.

Maddie moved to the sink and grabbed the sprayer attachment. "Nope, still knocking. And I need to get cooking, which means I'm giving you the count of three to clear on out of here. One. *Two*."

The lovebirds drew apart, laughing as they passed through the swinging doors.

"Three," Maddie said to an empty room. She returned the sprayer to its base with a sigh. That'd been more work than she'd anticipated, and even after all that fussing she hadn't been able to get Cole the advance. Though, if she was being honest with herself, she'd known her chances of getting that were slim to none. At least now she could say she tried. Hopefully, he'd understand and let it go. Besides, what could he possibly need fast cash for, anyway?

That look Miles and Stephanie had exchanged resurfaced in her mind. Surely they were overreacting about Cole not wanting a FITS job. So what if he'd backed away from the suggestion that he apply—didn't mean the guy had skeletons worth hiding in his closet.

Right?

She pictured Cole as he looked in the kitchen last night, with his warm smile and laid-back demeanor. Her gut was telling her the others' concerns were all wrong, that her new dishwasher/potential dating coach was as innocent as anyone. Then again, her gut had led her down the wrong path before.

Maddie still had the emotional scars to prove it.

...

Cole sensed a change the minute he stepped into the Checkerberry's kitchen that night. Not just in the aroma permeating the room—some kind of beef brisket instead of ham, and mouthwatering at that—but something else. A change he was all too familiar with but had done his darnedest to leave back in Texas. And though Maddie offered the same distracted nod she'd given him in parting last night, her eyes followed his movement as he crossed the room to grab a clean apron. Which meant the monkey that had been mercifully absent these past few months had found his back yet again: suspicion.

"Was beginning to wonder if you'd come back," she said.

"Why, expected me to skip town?"

"What?" She looked up from a bowl of potatoes she was peeling, dark brows furrowed. "No, I just have a bit of a reputation, is all. Guess for once it didn't precede me."

Talk about ironic. He thought she was being suspicious of him, and it was actually the other way around. Maybe his tarnished track record hadn't caught up with him yet after all. If he played his cards right, it never would. He'd been unfairly charged, done time that never should have been given. And all because he'd forever ago swapped parental roles with his addict mother and wound up in the wrong place at an even worse time.

Life more than owed him a do-over. Who knew—maybe Maddie would help kick-start it.

"Oh?" he asked, playing innocent though he'd been to enough Sunday luncheons over the summer here to know exactly what she meant. If the Checkerberry's chef wasn't happy, she did little to hide it. "And what reputation would that be?"

She brushed past him, snipping nothing but air with kitchen sheers as she moved. "That I'm a pain to work with. Mouthy, bull-headed, brash."

"Now you tell me."

Their gazes met and both broke into a grin.

"You get me my raise?" he asked.

"Depends. You actually gonna wash some dishes tonight

or just stand there yapping?"

Sweet. Resisting the urge to do a fist pump, he ambled toward the sink. Surely he could survive that sharp tongue of hers by working hard and staying in her good graces.

"Moving that slow will get you nowhere quick, Granville."

If she had any good graces…

"And my advance?" he asked.

"Work first, talk later."

What was with her being intentionally vague about his cash? She wouldn't try to pull one over on him, not after seeming so pleased with his work last night. Would she? "You're the boss, boss."

Cole reached into the sink, then quickly yanked his hand back out of the water. Good lord, the woman was either bent on killing bacteria or singing the skin off his hands!

He turned on the faucet, adding cold water to the mix, and tried to ignore the way his skin felt like it was still on fire. Maddie walked past, arched a brow at the running water, and reached for her radio. A few button taps later, '90s alternative rock was suddenly alive and well.

He eased a hand into the soapy water, found it to be slightly under 1,000 degrees this time, and set to work. Behind him, Maddie settled back into whatever routine he'd interrupted. He snuck a glance now and then, more to see if he could catch her hawk-eyeing him again. To his relief, she seemed to have more or less forgotten he was even there.

And to his enjoyment, her back was often to him. A view he'd never scoff, as she had some amazing curves. Maddie wasn't one of those toothpicks of a woman like the ones plastered all over billboards and television commercials. Her work clothes weren't overly flattering, the angles designed to conceal not highlight, but they didn't hide everything. Besides, he knew better after first spying her outside of work a few months back at the laundromat across the street. He'd done a double take, hardly recognizing her in a long dark sweater and jeans. Judging by the way she always kept to herself there, Maddie didn't seem to be much of a social butterfly — which explained the dating pinch she'd admitted to being in yesterday.

Of course, if she had any clue of the effect a body like that could have on the vast majority of Michigan's male population, she wouldn't need a stitch of coaching. As if to taunt him, she chose that moment to open the oven and slide a dish inside, bending low to keep its contents from spilling. If they'd been in Texas, he'd be whistling.

"Stop looking at my butt, Granville."

The small glass bowl in his sudsy grip slipped and he scrambled to catch it before it fell back into the water and landed on a number of other breakable items. "No idea what you're talking about."

"Uh-huh." She finished with the oven and came over to dump a handful of freshly dirtied utensils in the water. "Next you're going to say you were assessing my assets to help prep me for our first coaching session."

The woman was brilliant. Snarky as hell but brilliant. He'd take a bailout any day. "You're a quick learner."

"Not quick enough."

She turned away with a frown and Cole opened his mouth to ask why. But when she picked up a knife and started not-so-quietly dicing onions and peppers, he reconsidered. Maybe another time, when she wasn't wielding a lethal weapon.

And wait — had she just admitted that they'd soon be having their first coaching session?

The swinging doors that led out to the dining room scraped the floor behind him, the sound followed by a startled coo. He turned to find a young woman in skinny jeans and a tight V-neck with the word PINK stretched across her meager chest. She stared at him with mouth ajar, a white piece of gum teetering precariously on her tongue.

"What's he doing here?"

Cole looked to a frowning Maddie, who, after an awkward moment of silence, set her knife down with a sigh.

"What are *you* doing here, Sarah?" she asked.

"It's Thursday—I always come in around this time on Thursdays."

"Well, that's partially correct," said Maddie. "You did use to come in around now—which, by the way, is *late*—on Thursdays. But that was before you put your social life ahead of your responsibilities here for the last time."

"I really don't think we should be talking about this in front of"—Sarah waved a hand in Cole's direction—"him."

"'Him' has a name, actually." Maddie walked over to place a hand on his shoulder. The touch, though anything but intimate, jolted him like a giant zap of static electricity and warmed him from head to toe. "Sarah, this is Cole. Unlike you, he's punctual, courteous, and highly efficient. Oh, and I'm pretty sure he won't be walking out on me like you did, chasing after some bozo named Mark."

"It was Matt," Sarah said through clenched teeth.

"Nope," said Cole. "I won't be chasing after one of those, either."

Maddie let go of his shoulder to offer him a fist bump. Sarah, however, looked less than amused.

"That's my job, and you promised I could work here until the end of the season."

"That was before you walked out on me yesterday. For future reference? That's called insubordination, and I'm *preeeeeetty* sure that'll get you fired from about 99.9 percent of the jobs out there." Maddie turned from the girl and walked back to her cutting board. "Speaking of which, good luck finding the next one. Hope Mark was worth it."

With a frustrated roar, Sarah spun on her heel and slammed

her way out through the swinging doors. Cole watched her go, wide-eyed. Was that how people were brought up to act in Michigan? Back home, he would have gotten a belt to his backside for behaving like that.

He turned to Maddie, realization settling in. She could have sent him packing, allowed Sarah to resume her post, and gone back to the way things were. This was her kitchen to run, as she so often reminded him yesterday. Instead, she'd stood her ground and defended his presence. When was the last time anyone besides his grandfather had done that?

A quick glance found her dragging a hand down one side of her face. He wished there was something he could do to repay her for her kindness, to ease her burden. But all he had to offer was music and humor. Without his guitar, humor would have to do.

"I think it was Matt," he whispered.

She looked over and met his gaze, a weary smile tugging at her lips.

"Oh, I know. Knew it all along. Also knew the jerkwad wasn't good for her, but clearly she never listened to a word I said."

He leaned against the sink. "So let me get this straight. You seem to have a good sense of how other people's relationships will go, and yet you're struggling to find a date for this fancy dance of yours?"

Her full lips formed a small *O* and pink crept into her cheeks. "I...something like that."

"Uh-huh."

"New rule—no talking dating stuff until after the dinner rush." Maddie picked up her knife and wagged it in his direction.

He raised both hands in surrender and turned back to his dishes. "Yes, ma'am."

"*Maddie.*"

Cole chuckled. Oh yeah, he had to get her set up with the guy from the laundromat now. Not just because he enjoyed watching his over-confident boss squirm any time the subject of dating came up, but because he owed her. Big time. To defend him like that was about the biggest gift anyone had given him in a long, long time.

So while she focused on dinner preparations, he did his due diligence at the sink, savoring the aromas wafting through their shared space. Beef, vegetables, freshly baked bread. A person could gain ten pounds just from the smells in a kitchen like this. And though he told himself not to get his hopes up for another meal handout, Cole was happy as a pig in slop when she later slid a plate full of brisket and mixed vegetables his way.

"Thanks," he said, reaching for a fork.

"No thanks necessary. Just trying to fatten you up, is all."

She shifted from one foot to the other, her gaze anywhere but his. Cole felt his appetite begin to slip. *Here it comes, the brush off...*

"So, Cole, I know we talked about your salary requirements last night..."

"Yes."

"And I want you to know it was no easy task to get approval for an increase like that. Like, not at all."

He studied her face, still unreadable. "But you got it, right?"

"I did. Though, I honestly can't say for how long. We're only open until the end of November, and even then, if business starts to decline Miles will insist we start cutting expenditures."

"Meaning staff."

She shrugged. "Among other things."

Okay, so a few weeks at the worst, a month and a half at the most. He ought to be able to build up a decent student roster by then. "And my advance?"

"That I did not get."

Cole cursed under his breath. Two nights now he'd wasted here, in the hopes of getting the cash he needed, when he should have been out hunting for odd jobs that would pay on the spot. He drew his ball cap off, smoothed a hand over his hair, and set the cap back in place—a motion that usually helped trigger fresh ideas. Tonight, it brought him nothing.

"Can I ask you something?" Maddie's voice was softer now, less prickly than usual. Cole looked up but remained quiet, still too angry at the unexpected turn of events to speak. "What do you need it for?"

He stabbed at his dinner and took another bite. Somehow, the dish had lost its flavor. "Does it matter?"

"Humor me."

Been there, done that, and look where it got me.

He pushed the plate away. "For a deposit. On a storefront downtown."

"A storefront?"

"A guitar shop, actually, for doing repairs and giving lessons. Been eyeing a few places since I moved to town, but didn't think any of the leases would be up for another six months or so. The one with the most potential became available yesterday."

"Let me guess—they want a deposit."

"Bingo. I've been saving all summer, working odd jobs wherever I can. But I'm still short."

All that blood, sweat, and tears had been for nothing. And the hundred he'd put down on it this morning to lock in his chance at the place in anticipation of having the rest in hand tomorrow from Maddie? Apparently that'd been all for nothing, too. Cole felt his anger shift to another emotion he'd grown all too familiar with over the past few years: defeat. He pinched the bridge of his nose, using the pain to distract him from his growing disappointment.

"By two hundred bucks," she said.

"Yeah. By two hundred bucks."

A small thump sounded on the counter, and a paper-clipped stack of greenbacks slid in to view. He stared at it for a long moment, not quite believing what he was seeing. Maddie's shoes issued a soft squeak as she busied herself collecting dirtied dishes in her workspace, drawing him out of his shock.

"What's this?"

She brought an armload of dishes to the sink and carefully dropped them into its soapy depths. "Let's just say you aren't the only one who ever dreamed of striking out on their own."

A lump formed in his throat. "Maddie, I can't take this."

"Sure you can."

"No, I—"

She planted a hand on one hip. "You want to keep working here or not?"

"Well, sure."

"Then you'll take it already and shut up about it."

"But it could take me months to pay you back!"

Maddie shrugged. "How about you get me a date for this stupid gala and we'll call it even. Deal?"

Cole couldn't believe his ears. His dreams of starting his own business, of finally landing in a good community where he could set down roots and become a contributing member of society, were finally within his grasp. All because of Maddie's unexpected—and completely voluntary—act of kindness.

That made two in as many days. He fought the urge to reach out and pull her into a tight embrace, to whisper his thanks in her ear; it wasn't what a new employee or even a relationship coach should do. Still, he couldn't help but feel a bit jealous of this guy she'd set her sights on. He was a lucky man indeed.

"Deal."

Chapter Five

Maddie climbed the steps to her apartment Sunday afternoon, her body weary but mind a whirlwind of thoughts. Today was Cole's first day off from kitchen duty since he'd started, and she'd really looked forward to having the kitchen all to herself again. It'd always been her safe haven, a fortress where she could keep her mind busy and heart safe from harm. Working alongside scrumptious Cole, though, had rattled her more than she cared to admit. So a day with the space all to herself had sounded like a wonderful thing.

Until she walked into the inn's silent kitchen this morning, that is. She'd sauntered in, put her things away, and pulled on a fresh apron just like every other morning. And yet something felt off. It wasn't until Cole popped his head through the swinging doors "just to say hi" on his way to play guitar for the inn's Sunday service that she identified what that "off" was:

It was *him*.

Or, rather, today's lack thereof.

Which was stupid, of course. He'd never even worked the

breakfast or lunch shifts with her. In fact, most days he didn't stroll in until around three forty-five. But for some unknown reason, the idea of him not being there this evening had left her feeling a bit blue.

"Ridiculous."

She shoved the key into her apartment's doorknob, jiggled it a bit to coax the lock to cooperate, then twisted hard left and shouldered the creaky beast open. There was no way she was going to let herself go and get attached to Cole Granville, not now and not ever. He was too smooth, too handsome, and had a background she knew next to nothing about.

But darn it if his smile today hadn't triggered an unprompted smile of her own.

Maddie rubbed her stinging shoulder as she crossed the room, and made a note to hit her bum of a landlord up again about oiling the lock and hinges. She was fresh out of WD-40, and it was his job to fix things, anyway, not hers. With a shake of her head, she tossed her purse and keys down, and sank onto the barstool before her fishbowl.

"Hey, Fido."

Her goldfish perked up, his mouth moving in double-time as he bonked the side of the bowl nearest his container of fish food.

"Yeah, I know, buddy, you're hungry. You're always hungry." She chuckled. "Goofball fish."

Maddie humored him with a few small flakes, then leaned onto the countertop, propping her head in one hand to watch him. So maybe a goldfish hadn't been the pet she'd really wanted. An apartment the size of a postage stamp over a used bookstore in downtown Mount Pleasant instead of owning a place of her own—one with a modern kitchen, a reliable stove, and its own washer and dryer—hadn't been in her original plans, either. But if giving up what she really wanted meant running her own kitchen at a place she loved to work, well, these were small prices to pay. After all, she had heat in the winter and window-unit air conditioning in the summer—what more did she really need?

Not that extra two hundred dollars she'd given to Cole, apparently. She was still trying to come to terms with how readily she'd handed the money she'd been paid Thursday afternoon for her latest catering side job at the Women's Club over to him. Like it'd been burning a hole in her pocket—which, of course, it wasn't. With the items she needed to replace around her apartment, she'd had no intention of paying him the advance. But the way he'd looked at her upon realizing the money wasn't coming... Maddie shook her head to clear that kicked puppy look from her mind. Whatever his mysterious past held, that look of defeat Thursday night whispered it probably hadn't been nearly as cozy as hers.

"So I helped the guy out," she said to Fido. "Is that so wrong?"

Fido bumped into the side of the bowl a few times.

"No, he's not going to be my new pet project. I learned from the last one, I told you that."

An unwanted memory surfaced, of her college days and time spent studying in her apartment. Under the covers. With Harrison Essex.

Harrison, who was by far the cutest guy in her intermediate pastries class.

Harrison, who had cozied up to her. Made her believe he cared about her, was attracted to her.

Harrison, who had sweet-talked her into his bed...then dropped her like a hotcake the minute their semester ended and he'd passed with flying colors.

"Oh, come on, Madelyn. You know you're not really my type." His ice blue eyes had scanned her up and down. *"Or my preferred size."*

God, that'd hurt.

Heck, it'd more than hurt—it darned near killed her. She'd grown up with very little in the way of self-confidence. So to be tossed aside by her first real boyfriend, used and discarded without care? Those were dark days she never wanted to experience again. Ever.

Too bad her current boss was a white-haired cupid who'd run out of grandsons to play matchmaker with. Her hints to Maddie about every single guy between here and Lake Michigan had been getting less disguised by the day. Thus the lie. Which meant if she didn't secure a date to Miles and Stephanie's darned gala soon, things were sure to get dicey.

"No way am I going to sit back and let that happen."

Her gaze slid to the front window. Across the street stood the Quarter Clean-It, where Cute Guy would likely visit sometime today. The guy went through gym clothes faster than anyone she knew, not that Maddie was complaining—it meant he did laundry two or three times a week.

Yeah, she'd been counting. Yes, she took small loads of her own over there on the off chance one of these days she'd catch his eye and actually strike up a decent conversation. Maybe now that Cole was onboard with coaching her in the wild world of dating, she could cut to the chase and make fewer trips.

Maddie stood and crossed the room, staying back from the window so people on the sidewalk below wouldn't see her. Sure enough, in the near corner was Cute Guy, sitting in his usual chair, back to the rest of the place, one ankle resting atop his opposite knee and a magazine she'd bet money on was of the body builder variety in his hands. He was everything she wasn't—fit, tall, slender—and yet she felt inexplicably drawn to him. Like he was her holy grail or something. Being around him scrambled her thoughts and triggered gratuitous daydreams that usually managed to push work off her mind.

Which meant if anyone could clear her head of Cole

Granville and the insane idea that she was becoming at all attached to him, Cute Guy could do it.

A knock sounded at her door, breaking her concentration. Maddie frowned. She wasn't expecting anyone today.

The landlord! She snapped her fingers and headed for the door.

"You finally come to fix these hinges?" she called, struggling to get the blasted thing open. With a grunt and strong tug, she loosed it from its place of rest. The door flung open, leaving a clear view of the visitor on her doorstep. A visitor who was definitely *not* her landlord.

Yes, they were both male. But the guy standing before her now wore a contagious grin, a black fitted T-shirt beneath a denim jacket, and frayed jeans that hung oh-so-nicely on a pair of slender hips. A far cry from her middle-aged, droopy pantsed, combover-haired landlord.

"Nope." Cole shifted his laundry basket higher on one hip. "I came over to help fix you up."

"What, right now?"

"No time like the present. Besides, that beefcake you told me about is doing his laundry. Don't want to miss our window of opportunity."

"Window of opportunity?" Oh man, what had she gotten herself into? It was one thing, throwing smiles at Cute Guy from across the room, but to actually talk to him with Cole there watching? What would she say? What should she wear?

What if she threw up in mid-sentence?

"We don't have all day, Madds. Just grab a basket with a few things in there and let's go."

"But I'm not ready! I...I..." She raised both hands to her burning cheeks. "What if he doesn't like what's in my basket?"

"He's a guy. Guys don't think like that. They like pretty faces and...well, we'll get to the rest eventually. Today, the goal is to get his attention. A little smiling, maybe exchange names. Easy peasy. Now go get a basket."

"Easy peasy." She stormed to retrieve her laundry basket and made sure there wasn't anything too damning inside before returning to Cole. "What if it goes further than that? What if he starts talking to me? Asking questions?"

"Then you talk to him, answer his questions, just like we're doing now. You're not on the verge of a nervous breakdown talking to me, are you?"

Maddie swallowed hard. "No. But—"

"No buts. Just…do what comes naturally."

Oh, sure, do what comes naturally. Piece of cake…for someone like him. She ran a hand over her hair. "What if it doesn't work? What if he doesn't even notice me?"

"Trust me, he will. But on the off chance he doesn't, drop something."

"Drop something?"

Cole grinned, pretended to drop something, then slowly reached for the imaginary item, wiggling his butt as he went.

"Oh, you are terrible, Cole Granville."

"No, I'm male." He stepped around her to coax the door shut. "So follow my lead, and you'll have this date for your dance in no time."

She pictured Cute Guy, all six foot something and ripped. Her, bend over in front of him? The guy would probably volunteer to enroll her at his gym, not suggest they do dinner and a movie.

Maddie looked to the staircase, wondering how badly it would hurt if she accidentally on purpose missed the first step and took a tumble. Because with as persistent as Cole was being, it'd take a trip to the ER to get her out of this excursion. Who knew, maybe a good old-fashioned concussion wouldn't be so bad?

• • •

Cole picked a washer across the nearly empty laundromat from where Maddie's crush sat and began fishing a handful of quarters from his pocket. Silly girl had been practically hyperventilating by the time they reached Quarter Clean-It's front door. Why, he had no idea. Maddie was a lioness in the kitchen—why should the laundromat be any different?

Sure, she wasn't exactly dressed to the nines right now in jeans and a baggy black shirt, but anyone with a pulse would see the curves she hadn't managed to hide today and know there were more where those came from. And her hair was pulled up into one of those cute, messy buns, leaving little pieces to fall and curl around her neck and face. Between that and her flawless complexion, Muscles would be an idiot not to at least give her the time of day.

Though, if she didn't speak up soon, maybe he wouldn't.

A quick glance proved she hadn't bolted for the door. Hadn't done anything yet, actually. Instead, she stood frozen a few machines away from her target, Muscles, body rigid and basket in a death grip. Her gaze slid to Cole's. He gave her a nod and motioned for her to go on, then leaned a hip on his own machine and crossed his arms. Message received, she turned back to the far corner and slinked forward.

Watching her draw close to the guy, Cole couldn't help but wonder what it was about Muscles that had Maddie gunning for him in the first place. Sure, he was clean cut and in shape, and broad—the guy's chest had to have been twice as wide as Cole's—but there had to be something else. Something that'd attracted her to him. Surely someone like her, a take-charge kind of woman, would never go for a guy on looks alone. She'd need someone with a spine, someone to spar with who wouldn't easily back down.

Maybe, he wondered, as Maddie set her basket atop the machine next to her target's and Muscles didn't look up from his magazine, she'd set her sights on that guy because he was a challenge. Now that was more likely. It also potentially made his own promised coaching job a bit more difficult.

She glanced toward Muscles and offered the guy a shy smile.

It was lost on him, his attention yet focused on that magazine.

Maddie slid a hand into her front pants pocket, the move more provocative than likely intended. Cole swallowed hard and looked momentarily back to Muscles, who was still oblivious to the show going on before him. Cole fought the urge to go over and smack him upside the head.

She began plunking coins into the machine.

Muscles still didn't look up.

The water kicked on, and Maddie added detergent.

Still nothing.

She planted a hand on her hip.

You've got to do something else, something to really get his attention.

As if she'd heard his thoughts, Maddie began bending over very slowly, reaching for her basket. A coin slipped loose from her hand, and hit the floor with a metallic ping.

"Oops."

Muscles looked up. *Finally*.

"Drop something?"

Cole rolled his eyes. Yep, she'd picked a brilliant one. Though, who was he to judge?

Maddie flashed Muscles an embarrassed smile. "Yeah, just a quarter. Guess I've got butter fingers today."

He nodded. "Need some help?"

"Help?" Her smile slipped a little. "Oh, uh, no. I can get it."

Cole watched her drop to her knees and reach under the machine in search of her lost coin. With a silent groan he turned away, trying to prevent the image from burning into his memory. Darn it, why'd he have to go and start working for a woman with killer curves like that? He'd always been a sucker for curvy women. Back home, they'd been all about him, too. Though, seeing as he and his mama hadn't stayed in any one place long enough to grow roots, Cole's experiences with girls his age were quick and fleeting. Probably a good thing—it kept them away from the trouble that followed him like a shadow.

It had, anyway, until Old Tom had come to Texas and rescued him this spring.

Cole drew in a deep breath, his gaze drifting to the laundromat's picture window. Two blocks over stood the storefront that could help him build a future in this town, more so than helping a grandfather who didn't truly require any help. But the guitar shop, that would be Cole's own. His pride and joy, his contribution to society. A society that had yet to shun him, had yet to discover the truth about his past. He hoped like mad it would stay that way.

"Um, excuse me? Might need that help after all."

He turned toward the sound of Maddie's voice, more muffled than it'd been the last time she'd spoken, and was surprised to see her still down on all fours. Only now her face was red, and her sheepish look replaced with one far more... angry.

Muscles set his magazine down and sprang from his seat. Words were exchanged, and still she remained on the floor. He stood, grabbed two corners of the washer, and tried lifting. Judging by his red-faced grunting and scowl, it hadn't budged. He repositioned his feet so that he had one on each side of her hips. Maddie hung her head, shaking it back and forth.

Oh no.

Cole hurried across the room to offer his assistance. Though, with as well as his first piece of advice had turned out, Maddie may well not accept any more. Heck, if she was half as mad as he sensed, she might well fire him the moment they step outside. Which he absolutely could not let happen if he wanted to keep his dream shop open longer than a month.

It'd been a dream too long in the making for him to stand back and let that happen.

Chapter Six

Cole watched Maddie stalk by without so much as a sideways glance for the hundredth time Tuesday night and sighed. He'd been given the cold shoulder a lot in his lifetime, but never by a boss, and never in close quarters like this. Which was a total bummer, as he'd looked forward to telling her about his meeting with Sheridan Realty this afternoon—and how his dream was so close to becoming reality now he could nearly taste it.

Too bad tonight's menu had been full of nothing but sour grapes.

"Oh, come on, Maddie. You can't stay mad at me forever."

More silence. At least this time, it was accompanied with eye contact. Though, if looks could kill…

"Look, I said I was sorry like, what, a million times now? How many more will it take for you to forgive me?"

She planted a hand on one hip, her lips pursed so tight he was nearly afraid to hear what was stored behind the floodgate. After glaring at him for another excruciatingly long moment, she drew closer, fire in her eyes. "Another million.

And next time you have a bright idea? Count me out."

Okay, so that was progress. Cole made a mental note to do his best not to tick her off again.

"I'm sorry, I'm sorry, I'm so—"

"Gah, enough." She threw her hands up and spun on her heel to grab a wineglass from the drying rack. "Just let it go already."

He watched her pace back over to the refrigerator, hoping she wasn't going for more wine. His first week on the job, she hadn't touched a drop. Tonight, she'd tapped into her cheap boxed wine at least twice. Already, her eyes were looking a bit glassy. Thankfully, the cooking was done, and the two of them were focused solely on cleanup. But much more, and he worried she wouldn't be in any shape to drive.

How many times had he watched his mother do the same? Get stupid on drinks, stupid on drugs? A kid can only pretend to look the other way so many times, especially when the consequences start landing on the wrong person's shoulders.

To his dismay, Maddie withdrew from the fridge with her glass again half full of white zinfandel. Cole hated jeopardizing their already-strained relationship, but he hated even more the idea of her splattered on the side of the road somewhere. He tossed his towel down and walked over to where she stood.

"What are you doing?"

She paused with the glass at her lips, eyebrows raised. "Getting a drink, what does it look like?"

"Then have a glass of water."

"It's not as tasty." She took in his flat look and tightened her grip. "I have a glass or two when I'm stressed. My kitchen, my rules."

"I don't care if it's the president of the United States's kitchen—much more and you're not gonna make it home in one piece."

She snorted. "Good, then I won't have to look as hard for a new place to do my laundry."

She was stalling, trying to sidestep his intervening ways. He'd seen it a million times. Unlucky for her, he also knew about a million ways to get around it.

"It wasn't that bad," he said, keeping his voice casual. "Tyson knows your name now, and you know his."

"Yep, he sure does. I'll forever be known as 'Maddie Whose Fat Arm Got Stuck Under a Washer' to him. Terrific."

"Since when did you become the pouty, mopey type?"

Her eyes widened with surprise. "What?"

"You heard me."

"For your information, I am neither pouting nor moping." She slammed her glass down.

Bingo.

Cole swiped it off the counter, marched to the sink, and dumped its contents down the drain. He turned back to find her wide-eyed face turning redder by the second.

"What did you do that for?"

"For your own good."

"And who's the boss in here?"

"You are." Cole yanked his apron off and slammed it into the laundry hamper. "But that doesn't mean I'm going to stand around and watch you get hammered. Unlike you, my work is done."

Her scowl deepened. "Good. Go home so you don't have to watch."

"Fine."

He passed by the fridge to grab his coat, then came back to it, swiped the box of wine, and turned for the swinging double doors.

"Where the heck do you think you're going with that?"

"Home," he said without looking back. "So I don't have to watch."

He slammed through the doors, startling Ruby and Kayla who were folding napkins at the bar that separated the kitchen from the dining room. Maddie's shouts followed in bursts as the doors swung open and shut in his wake. The women looked from the kitchen to him to the object in his hands. A knowing smile dawned on Ruby's face.

"Heading home, dear?"

"Yes, ma'am."

She rose from her seat, giving Kayla's arm a reassuring pat, then turned her attention to him. "I'll see you out."

"That's not necessary, Mrs. Ma—"

"Don't you Mrs. Masterson me, Cole Granville. It was Ruby the day you were born and it'll be Ruby until the day you die."

Now it was Kayla's turn to grin. She ducked her head and said her farewells as they passed by. Ruby lay a gentle hand upon Cole's arm as they made their way to the lobby.

"You really don't need to trouble yourself walking me out."

"Oh, I know. I also know the last thing you need is to have a partially consumed box of wine in your grandfather's truck." She gestured toward her office. "Leave it under my desk, dear. I'll have Brent put it back in the fridge in the morning."

"I had just planned on throwing it away, to be honest. I don't drink the stuff."

"Oh, now, don't go thinking poorly of our Maddie. We all have our flaws. Sometimes we just need a bit of help avoiding self-destruction by those closest to us now and then."

Cole knew full well about trying to keep people closest to him from self-destructing. He also knew how much of a lost cause for some people that could be.

"You think she'll be okay to drive home?"

"How many glasses did she have?" Ruby asked.

"Two that I saw, could have been more."

"Then Kayla and I will delay her, give the drink time to wear off. It's the cheap stuff, shouldn't take long." Ruby patted his arm once more, her eyes crinkled at the corners from her smile. "You're a good boy, Cole. Set that box in my office, then run on home to your grandfather and give him my regards."

"Yes, ma'am."

He stepped into Ruby's office, careful not to trip over the chairs set opposite her grand desk in the muted light, and set the box where she'd instructed. He rose to his full height and spied a nearby photo album, opened to an autographed picture of a former golf celebrity. Arnold Palmer, maybe? Curiosity drew Cole closer to flip through a few more pages, in awe at the idea of being in the same building as any of the pictured sports celebrities, movie stars, and politicians.

Ruby was one lucky lady. One of the kindest he knew, too. He trusted that she would take care of Maddie and see that she made it home safe and sound. But would she help cool his boss down enough to keep him from losing his job? Stealing her wine was right up there with insubordination, and he knew how strongly she felt about that—just ask Sarah.

He strode out the front door, shaking his head at how something like a simple kitchen job was beginning to turn his world upside down. *Not the job*, a voice in the back of his mind whispered. *The woman.*

Cole paused on the porch's bottom step and looked back to the inn. Why *had* he gotten all protective of Maddie tonight? She was a grown woman, old enough to make her own decisions, good, bad, or otherwise. So why had he stepped in and cut her off?

Because they were becoming friends, he realized, and that's what friends did. They also forgave each other when things didn't turn out as planned. Hopefully, she was beginning to consider him a friend, too. If she didn't…well, he'd just have to get over it. What other choice did he have?

Disappointed at how the night had gone, he continued on to his grandfather's truck. There wasn't anything he could do to make things better between him and Maddie tonight, so it was best to let it go and give her time to calm down. In the meantime, he'd just work on design sketches for his new shop and hope for the best.

• • •

Maddie finished her prep for tomorrow's breakfast in record time, anger speeding her actions.

Who did that jerk think he was, taking off with her wine like that? And tossing in a guilt trip about drinking and driving to boot? An insult to her character, as she'd never do something that stupid.

She threw a load of towels into the wash, swapped her apron for her purse, and headed for the swinging doors. It'd been a long night, and one she was more than ready to have end. Kayla and Ruby looked up from their seats at the bar top, appraising looks on each of their faces. Maddie drew to a temporary halt, feeling a sense of betrayal.

"Really? Just like that, you're going to take his side?" Both of them returned to their linen napkin folding, eyebrows raised but without retort. "Wow, and I thought women always stuck together when it came to guy issues."

"Are you having guy issues?" Kayla looked up. "I thought Cole was just your hired help."

"Well, yeah. Of course that's all he is."

"Hired help who was concerned about your general welfare, dear." Ruby set a completed napkin aside. "A far more noble gesture than your former staff ever offered. Such a disappointment, that one."

"Don't be too disappointed—I knew within five minutes of Cole being in the kitchen that he'd end up working rings around her. But this weekend he…"

What could she say? Admit he was helping coach her on dating? No, that'd defeat the whole purpose of her arrangement with Cole. She was trying to protect her ego, not dash it in front of the others. Maddie ran a hand over her hair, wishing she'd never lied. Stupid gala…

"You wanna talk about it?" asked Kayla.

"No." Which wasn't true. She'd bottled up her anger all day, carried it with her everywhere. Venting here among friends would bring her more peace than chewing Cole out. Too bad talking about it would require more lies, because no way was she coming clean on this whole coaching deal. She dropped into a chair near the others with a sigh. "Fine. He made me look like an idiot in front of Tyson Sunday."

"Tyson?" Kayla offered her a coy grin. "Who's Tyson?"

Crap. Well, now she really had to make sure she got a date with him for the gala, or her whole gig would be up. "My…the guy I'm sort of…"

"You have a *boyfriend*? When did this happen?" Kayla scooted her chair closer. "We need deets! Now spill."

This. This was why it was best around here to stay in the kitchen, safe behind those swinging doors. Maddie picked up the proverbial shovel and began digging the hole she was in deeper. "Well, it's all fairly recent. I met him at the Quarter Clean-It."

"Oooh, a local." Kayla and Ruby exchanged a look. "College guy?"

"No." At least, not that she knew of. Crap, this was only going to go from bad to worse. Time to give some generics, then change the subject. "He's tall, cute, muscular. Anyway, Cole shows up and, uh, causes me to drop my change. I squat down to reach under the washer for it and my sweater gets caught on something. So there I am, butt in the air and arm stuck under the machine, looking like a total idiot in front of

Tyson."

Ruby's powder puff eyebrows pinched together. "Well, I'm sure Cole didn't mean for you to end up in such an unflattering position. Was there something else he did to upset you, dear?"

"Well, no, but…"

The image of Cole stretched out on the floor beside her, trying to use his cell phone's flashlight to assess the damage, drifted to mind. The look on his face hadn't been amusement but concern. Maybe even a little fear.

Fear of her reaction to the situation, and darn it if she hadn't gone and given him plenty of reason to think that way tonight.

Maddie groaned. "I did it again, I lost my temper. Ruby, why do I do that?"

"It's the way you're wired, Madelyn. But the more aware of it you are, the harder you can work to contain it in the future."

"Maybe." She shook her head, doubting very much she'd ever be able to fully control her temper. Yet another reason to stay tucked safely away in a kitchen—the pots and pans never got their feelings hurt when she ranted at them. "Guess I owe him an apology."

Kayla nodded. "Wait—you don't think he'll quit, too, do you?"

Panic clawed at Maddie. He wouldn't, would he? Leave her stranded like Sarah had?

Only, the panic she felt now was different than when Sarah had left. The two women had never said much to each other that wasn't work related; they'd never connected. But with Cole she'd begun to enjoy his company, looked forward to seeing him, spending time together with him. Heck, they'd even started playing name-that-tune on the radio each night during cleanup. Having fun.

For him to quit would cost her more than a staff member; it'd be losing a friend.

Ruby *tsk-tsked* as she leaned forward to give Maddie's hand a soft pat. "I'm sure he will cool down by morning, dear."

"You think?"

The innkeeper smiled. "If he's anything like his grandfather, he will. Besides, someone determined to quit wouldn't bother taking their boss's wine to keep her safe from harm, now would they?"

No, probably not. Still, the possibility nagged at her. She needed to talk to him, to apologize for being such a hothead and beg him to come back. And to thank him for looking out for her—something she wasn't used to anyone but the Mastersons doing for her. But when?

As usual, Ruby seemed to read her mind.

"Why don't you stop over there before the shop opens tomorrow?" the innkeeper said. "You're long overdue a morning off anyway, dear."

"Thanks, Ruby."

"Of course, dear. Though, it would be a great help if you could stay a bit longer tonight and help fold the rest of these napkins. I can't imagine how we ever got so far behind."

Kayla grinned, clearly sharing some secret with Ruby. Rather than ask, Maddie said she'd be happy to help and reached for a handful of the linen rectangles. Besides, listening to the others ramble about the goings-ons of the inn was a much better alternative to sitting at home, fretting about what she should say to Cole in the morning.

If, that was, he'd even give her the time of day. She looked back toward the dark kitchen and hoped like crazy he was a forgiving soul.

Kayla cleared her throat. "So, Maddie, tell us more about this Tyson guy…"

Chapter Seven

Cole sat in the hardware store's office Wednesday morning, staring at the computer screen in disbelief. He'd received an email from Sheridan Realty shortly after eight a.m., instructing him to fill out their standard online application in order to complete his lease request. Eager to knock that out, he had run downstairs and dug right in.

As the email had promised, it was a simple enough form. Address, phone number, emergency contacts, prior convictions or felonies…

Wait, *what*?

Cole re-read item number seven, then shoved back from the machine with a growl. Why? Why did it matter what his criminal record was? All he wanted to do was lease a storefront, bring some culture to downtown Mount Pleasant. Did it really matter that he'd seen the inside of a prison cell for far longer than he should have?

He bent to rest both elbows on his knees, fighting the urge to vomit. Or throw something. Maybe a little of both.

All those years he'd spent trying to look after his mom,

to keep her off the streets and out of harm's way. And how did she repay him? By falling off the wagon that last time, and falling *hard*. His failed rescue attempt had been warped into charges of armed robbery, and off to jail he'd gone. With no money for a lawyer, and then appointed what had to be the greenest public defender in all of Texas, jail is right where he stayed. Definitely not how he'd envisioned his eighteenth birthday going, or the following three birthdays after that. And though he'd served the time he'd been wrongfully mandated to do, and not once violated the three-years' probation that followed, here he was facing punishment yet again. It just wasn't fair.

"Problems, son?"

Cole turned to find his grandfather at the office door, steaming coffee mug in hand. He shook his head and pointed to the computer screen.

"I was a fool to think I'd ever have a chance at normal. Doesn't matter where I go, the past just keeps on following me. All thanks to my dear old ma."

His grandfather's gaze slid to the screen. He pulled a pair of bifocals from his front shirt pocket, slipped them onto his nose as he drew closer, then bent to read over Cole's shoulder.

"Ah. I should have known that'd be part of their application. That question's on just about everything nowadays." He studied the screen a moment longer, then stepped back to take a drink from his coffee. "How much did you say rent was each month?"

"Don't." Cole clicked off the web application and rose from the chair. "You've bailed me out more than enough as it is."

"Me signing the lease for you wouldn't be bailing you out, it'd be helping you finally get your feet on the ground. You say you'd earn well enough to cover the cost, correct?"

"I would, if I had a place to offer lessons. Maybe I should

talk to Brent, see if he can help me build a shack to set up on the outskirts of town. Far away from anybody who cares whether or not some dumb kid from Texas has a rap sheet."

Old Tom chuckled. "Not sure that place exists, son. Not in these parts, anyway. Maybe it's time to stop hiding from your past. Wrong or not, it's a part of who you are. Eventually word is going to get out. And then what will you do? Pack up and leave town?"

"Maybe. Or maybe I'll just work doubly hard to make sure no one ever has reason to go looking for my past."

A throat cleared nearby. Both men spun to find Maddie standing just outside the office door. What on earth was she doing here?

Oh God. She's gonna fire me. He looked to the ceiling. *Could this day get any worse?*

The moment that thought entered his mind, Cole wished it hadn't. Because as she stood there, looking about as uncomfortable as a minister in a whorehouse, a bigger worry took hold of his thoughts.

Just how much had she heard?

• • •

Maddie stood peering into the office at Granville Supplies, feeling like an unwanted intruder on a private family moment. Cole rose from the room's lone chair, looking like anything but a member of the hardware store staff in his usual bad boy attire of faded denim, black boots, and T-shirt combo. His grandfather, on the other hand, had on worn khakis and a button-down shirt with the sleeves rolled up. Even so, the resemblance between them, she realized for the first time, was striking. Especially with them both standing there, cross-armed with brows furrowed. Judging from the looks on their faces, whatever discussion they'd been having wasn't anything light and fluffy. Heck, judging from the daggers Cole's gaze had aimed at her, she half wondered if they'd been talking about her deplorable behavior last night.

She nearly turned tail and ran.

But her conscience kept her rooted in place. She owed him an apology, darn it, no matter how angry he was with her right now. And rightfully so. The poor guy tries to make good on his word to help hook her up and what does she do? Give him the cold shoulder and then bark at his attempts at a sincere apology, no less.

"Why, I've a chef in my shop, and during the breakfast rush, no less." Tom Granville's frown smoothed into a broad smile. "Landlord failing you again, sweetie?"

She grinned. Only someone as old and genuinely kind as Mr. Granville could get away with calling a woman sweetie in this day and age.

"Good morning, Mr. Granville. Actually, I was hoping to talk to Cole before his shift tonight." Her gaze flashed briefly to his. "If he wouldn't mind."

"Oh? My boy giving you trouble, Miss Maddie?"

"Trouble?" She shook her head. "No. Actually, I came to—"

"Deliver something." Cole's voice was unusually icy. "Grandpa, could you excuse us for a moment?"

Old Tom looked to him in surprise, then shook his head with a chuckle. "Kicked out of my own office. Never thought I'd see the day."

He trudged off, coffee in hand and a smile on his face. Well, at least one of the Granvilles was in a good mood today. Too bad for her it seemed to be the wrong one. The minute Tom closed the door, Cole spoke up.

"All right, let's get this over with."

Maddie swallowed hard. The guy was rather intimidating when he was ticked.

"Well, good morning to you, too."

His eyes narrowed. Dang, did he have to make this so hard on her? Apologies weren't exactly her specialty.

Food, however, was.

She reached into her shoulder bag. "I, uh, brought you something."

"Great. Let me guess: it's pink, and—"

"Pink? Wow, I sure hope not." She produced the small plastic container stuffed with her nearly world-famous monkey bread and held it out to him. "Though, that's a great idea for the next time I get hired to cater a baby shower."

Cole took the container and stared at it in silence for a long moment. "This…is why you came by?"

"No." Maddie wrung her hands together. "I came by to apologize. For the way I treated you last night. I knew it wasn't your fault, my sleeve getting caught like that, but you were the easiest scapegoat. That whole laundry episode brought back some really bad childhood memories—I, uh, got picked on a lot—and, well, I lost my cool." She swallowed hard, the rest of her apology coming out at barely more than a whisper. "I just hope you can forgive me."

He looked up, a mixture of disbelief and confusion on his brows. "You mean…you didn't come here to fire me?"

"Fire you?" She blew out the breath she'd been holding in a rush. "For what, caring too much about my well-being?"

Ever so slowly, Cole's trademark crooked grin tugged at his perfect lips.

"Though," she added. "If you ever suggest I drop something again, don't be surprised if I don't."

"So…we're good?"

Good? He might be. She, however, felt rather tortured standing so close to all his hunky handsomeness. Maybe she should have fired him and let Sarah come back, just to get her libido under control. Then again, spikes in her hormones might actually get her to speak up and ask Tyson to that stupid gala. She took a step back to give her a little more space from Mr. Far-Too-Tempting-And-Oh-Yeah-He's-My-Employee, pretending to check for something on the bottom of her shoe.

"Does that mean you'll forgive me for being a total bi-otch last night and come back to work?"

"Only if you forgive me for acting like your mother hen." He ran a hand over the back of his neck. "Sorry, guess I had some bad memories dredged up, too."

"Deal. And...I'll lay off the wine when you're around from now on."

Maddie extended her hand his way. Instead of shaking, he pulled her into a tight hug.

"I thought I'd lost your friendship last night," he whispered, his cheek resting atop her head. "Took me forever to fall asleep."

The pain in his voice surprised her even more than the unexpected contact. She wrapped her arms around him, breathing in his delicious scent, savoring his warmth, all the while telling herself not to get too used to this. He was talking friendship, and that's all they were meant to be. Even if he had just admitted to lying in bed last night, thinking about her.

"Nah," she said, rubbing circles along his back. "It'd take a whole lot more than stealing my wine to do that."

"Good." He drew back all too soon, then grabbed a jacket off the chair he'd vacated. "You eat already?"

"No. You?"

"Nope, and I'm starved."

"We could just eat the monkey bread I brought." She shrugged.

"No way, I'm saving that for later. Why don't we go grab a bite? I need to get out of here for a while, clear my head. We can work on our next plan of attack while we're there."

Plan of attack? Maddie didn't have the foggiest idea what

that was all about, but found herself liking the "we" part of it all a good deal.

"Yeah, all right. Where're we going?"

He motioned toward the door and threw her a devilish grin. "You'll see."

. . .

Cole held the door open to EAT, enjoying the look of utter mortification on Maddie's face as she stepped inside. He'd heard someone mention it after church a while back and had fallen in love with the place. No snooty or opinionated patrons here. With its grease-laden atmosphere, slowly decaying interior, and quickly deteriorating exterior, it was simply a place people went to, well, eat.

All except for Maddie, who looked like she'd rather lick the Checkerberry's floor clean than consume their food… which made it that much more amusing. He'd just consider it restitution for her behavior last night. She angled for a far corner, casting him a look over her shoulder that could have put a sumo wrestler six feet under, but came to a halt a few steps farther.

"*Brent?*"

A broad set of shoulders flinched to their left. Brent Masterson lowered his newspaper and turned reluctantly from his plate full of diner food at the bar.

"Uh, hey, Maddie. Cole. Fancy meeting you here."

"There is nothing fancy about this place." She scanned the long bar with a look of disgust, her gaze landing on the half-eaten meal before him. "Really? I work my butt off each and every day to provide quality food at the inn and this is what you choose?"

Brent looked to him for moral support, and Cole grimaced. The last thing he wanted to do was get into a fresh argument with her. Even so, he couldn't leave Brent hanging, not when he was one of the few long-timers in town who always treated him like just another one of the guys.

"How about we leave Brent to his meal, huh? I bet he's just here choking it down because he's missing Kayla. She's probably back at the inn covering for you, right?"

"Uh-huh." Maddie's gaze narrowed. "We're gonna have words later, Masterson. *Words.*"

With a shake of her head she continued on toward the far booth. Brent's shoulders sagged with relief. He mouthed the words "thank you" and turned back to his meal. Cole just chuckled and followed after his boss.

"Can't believe that man." Maddie slid into the far booth with a frown. "Can't believe you, either."

"Oh, come on, Maddie. You deserve a break from cooking. Let someone else do it for you today."

She leaned forward, her voice low. "Cooking is not what I would call what goes on behind that wall."

Cole grabbed a menu poking up from amid the slew of condiments on the window-side of the table and refrained from commenting back. He'd never admit to Maddie, but EAT was one of his favorite places to go in this town. Because it was close to campus, the younger crowd was migratory and oblivious to the town's newcomers. The older crowd—Brent notwithstanding— was mostly crotchety old men who were more interested in what grain and pork bellies were selling for than the town's recent additions to their general population. Which left Cole free to kick back without worry that his past might rise up and bite him in the rear.

He glanced at the menu, the debate brief between eggs, eggs, and more eggs and a plate full of flapjack carbs—he was in an eggs kind of mood today—and set it aside. Seeing the waitress busy with another customer, he turned his attention back to Maddie. She sat with her hands in her lap, looking out over the place.

"Already know what you want?"

"A bottle of Clorox." She met his gaze. "And maybe a blowtorch."

He burst out laughing. Maddie's scowl deepened, but the hint of a grin ghosted across her lips. Lips, he realized sitting so close to her, that were as perfectly curvy as the rest of her.

"Come on, it's not that bad."

"Is, too. Let someone else do the cooking for me." She snorted. "More like let someone else serve me up a heart attack on a plate. With friends like you, who needs enemies?"

So she considered him a friend, too. Cole felt a warmth wash over him he hadn't felt in a long time. Not since the early days, before his dad had disappeared. Back when they had a home. A yard. A neighborhood…

He swallowed hard and looked away, afraid if he thought about it too long the spell would be broken. "Friend, huh?"

"Well, it sounds better than subordinate, doesn't it? And since we're not at work but sitting here together…"

She cleared her throat, and Cole glanced up in time to see a pretty pink tint to her cheeks. Ah, but that was a thought he shouldn't be having. She'd just called him a friend. Barely a step up from coworker. Someone as stable and grounded as Maddie deserved a guy with those same characteristics.

"Yeah, friend will work," he said. "Sounds better than enemy, that's for sure."

Yep, he had enough of those already, all because of his jacked-up past, his crappy timing, and his stupid trusting heart. Best to focus on building a career, which started with getting his shop off the ground. If only he could find a way to do that without risking his future in Mount Pleasant. Because the more time he spent here, the more this quiet, conservative town was beginning to grow on him.

Footsteps approached, and soon EAT's aging, no-

nonsense waitress appeared at their table. "Morning. You folks ready to order?"

"Just a coffee for me," said Maddie. When the waitress raised a brow, she added, "Oh, I already ate."

Liar. Cole threw her a look. She raised her chin in challenge. He just rolled his eyes and ordered the western omelet and coffee. The waitress shuffled off and was back shortly with her coffee pot, the smell a bit burnt and acidic but caused his stomach to rumble nonetheless. Maddie just stared down at the steaming cup of Joe as though it were antifreeze that'd been set before her.

"It won't kill you, Madds."

She arched a brow. "Or maybe it will, and that's why you brought me here."

He laughed. She had that effect on him often, intentional or not. It was one of the things he liked about her. And another reason why he needed to get her squared away with Tyson. Because the more time he spent with Maddie, the more Cole found himself thinking about her. And that just wouldn't do.

"Now, where would the fun in that be? Besides, I promised I'd help set you up with Tyson. Hard to do if you're pushing up daisies."

Maddie sighed and slid a hand in through the handle of her mug. "Yeah, but if you killed me then I wouldn't have to worry about needing to find a date for that stupid gala, now would I?"

"Hmm, not unless there's an eternity full of them waiting for you Upstairs."

"And that'd be just my luck, wouldn't it?"

She groaned, and Cole couldn't help but grin. Maddie could complain all she liked, but he bet she'd look amazing all dressed up for this crazy gala. Some fitted dress, maybe in a dark blue or purple. Hair done up, makeup on, polished toes peeking out from some sexy, open-toed high heels. He'd just started imagining what it'd be like, sliding his hands around her waist on the dance floor, when she spoke back up.

"So, what's our next step, coach?"

"Next step?"

Cole ran a hand through his mess of hair. Sexy heels? Where had that line of thinking come from? Maybe bringing her to breakfast hadn't been such a good idea after all, not if it was going to cause his imagination to start down those paths. She was counting on him to set her up with someone else, for crying out loud. Which meant the best thing that could happen now would be for him to get her and this Tyson guy paired up and paired up fast. Because the sooner she was off the dating market, the easier it'd be to stop this crush he seemed to be developing on his boss before it went any further.

Too bad to properly coach her meant things would likely get tougher before they got better. Coaching required time to be put in. One on one time.

He grabbed his own mug and took a long, scalding drink.

"Talking," he said with a wince. "We've got to get you two talking. And I know just what you need to do."

Chapter Eight

Maddie stood in her bedroom, hands in hair and heart racing. What had she been thinking, letting Cole talk her into coming back here to help pick out what she should wear the next time she hit the Quarter Clean-It? That place was a hole in the wall where people went to do their laundry, not some swanky martini bar!

Thank goodness her apartment was mostly clean. Still, him coming over had her feeling seriously unsettled, just like when he'd first stepped foot in her kitchen. Apparently, nowhere in this town was sacred anymore.

Then again, after a few days, she'd more or less gotten over that. Sure, she thought of him often when he wasn't there, but only because she was bored. And maybe a little lonely. Cole seemed to cure all of that.

Funny, she'd been looking for kitchen help and found herself a new friend. With her limited supply, any additions were well worth holding on to. A fresh wave of guilt pummeled her at the thought of how crappy she'd been to him last night. Stupid fragile ego of hers. If he could get her set up with Tyson, maybe her introverted self would finally develop a spine in social settings.

"You gonna take all day in there or what?"

Or maybe not.

Maddie looked to the door and hollered back, "Give me a minute, will ya?"

Grumbling additional four letter words under her breath, she stalked to her closet and flicked through clothes on hangers. Black shirt. Black skirt. Black pants. Another black shirt.

Tell me you have something other than black in your wardrobe, Maddie. She'd thrown him a dark look at that greasy dump called EAT—*PUKE* was more like it—for that comment, but darn it if he hadn't been too close to correct. With a growl she snatched a charcoal gray V-neck sweater from the rack and headed for the living room.

"How about this?"

He looked up from his place on the barstool beside Fido and flashed her a smile. Darn it, if that wasn't maybe the best sight she'd seen in this place. The guy looked adorable when he smiled like that. Why on earth he wasn't dating was beyond her. Or maybe he was, and he'd just kept very quiet about it? Probably that.

His gaze roved over the sweater, then shifted to hers. "I thought you said you were going to prove you had something other than black back there?"

"What are you talking about? This is charcoal gray, buddy. Hardly black."

He rolled his eyes. "In case you hadn't noticed, Madds, I'm a guy. And to a guy, black, gray, very dark blue—they're all pretty much the same."

Oh, I've noticed, she thought, working to keep her face neutral and eyes on his. *In fact, I'm doing my darnedest not to think about that too much right now. Not a line I should cross, seeing as you're my relationship coach and all...*

"So what you're saying is guys expect girls to strut around like princesses in pinks and yellows?"

"No, what I'm saying is this: too much black makes you blend in with the scenery. You want to stand out, look approachable. And a bit less…goth."

"Goth?"

He grinned. She groaned and headed back to her room.

"Surely you have something else in this magic closet of yours that's got a little more color in it."

Oh no.

She spun to close the door behind her but it was too late—Cole was already across the threshold. But whatever mortification and discomfort she felt seemed to have no effect on him. He strode past her, face forward and gaze intent on the closet.

"Good thing I cleaned up this morning," she said.

Only then did he glance back and take a quick look around, confusion clear on his face. "Why's that?"

"Never mind."

Men. Totally clueless. It was no wonder she wasn't in a relationship. Her tolerance for obliviousness was about nil.

Cole assessed her clothing options, barely looking at one item before flipping to the next. He paused at a lavender scoop neck top with three-quarter sleeves. "See? Here, something like this."

"Um, no."

"Why not?"

"Because a neckline like that is not what a girl like me"—Maddie motioned toward her chest—"can wear if she's going to be repeatedly bending over a washing machine. I'll scare the other patrons."

"Or draw their attention." He waggled his brows.

She looked toward her bedroom window and squinted out at nothing. Cole just didn't understand. Some bodies were made for flaunting. Hers wasn't one of them. "That's not the kind of attention I want. Trust me."

"If you say so."

They went back and forth for several minutes like this, him throwing out ideas and her shooting them down. Clearly, he didn't understand body mechanics for the well-endowed. Or the thicker-than-average. Then again, why would he? The guy didn't have a scrap of excess on him. With a sigh, Maddie took a seat on the edge of her bed.

"Look, I appreciate your help, but maybe I'm not cut out for all of this. Not without a serious makeover and expensive shopping trips. Who has time for that?"

"Wait. This." Cole slipped a hanger from the rack and turned to show her his latest find. A teal camisole with lace-fringed top came into view. "You could wear it under the cardigan you have on."

She threw him a skeptical look. The cami was a bit on the clingy side, and Maddie preferred not to draw attention to her shape any more than necessary. Usually, she wore that item under a V-neck sweater, to help hold the girls in place and cover up what the "v" didn't.

"Oh, come on now, give it a chance. See? Not too gapey." He tugged at the neckline. "And the cardigan will hang loose over it. You'll have comfort with a pop of color. It's the best of both worlds."

"A pop of color?" She laughed. "Oh my gosh, you sound like the guys on HGTV."

A scarlet flush crept into his cheeks. "Yeah, well, maybe I've had to endure listening to those shows a time or two. Hard not to pick up a few things along the way."

Endured listening? There was a lot of Cole she didn't know about. Heck, she hardly knew anything about him, other than that he had an extremely high tolerance of her snarky ways. He hadn't bugged her to spill about her past, and she'd refrained from prying into his. Because if he was anything like her, he kept quiet about his past because it was best left there—in the past.

For now, she'd enjoy his company and try to be a good recipient of his coaching. If he could help her win over Tyson, maybe "bored" and "lonely" would gradually fall away from her routine-ruled life. She offered him a smile, as it was all she had to give.

"Then a pop of color it is."

• • •

Cole set his acoustic on its stand in the corner of his room, hating to end his practice session but knowing it was nearly time to head to the Checkerberry for his shift. A new song had been teasing his thoughts all day, something sweet with a bit of upbeat twang. Seems you could take a man out of Texas, but couldn't take the Texas out of a man…

"What'd you decide?"

Cole looked up, the three bars of music he'd been mulling over evaporating. "Sorry?"

"About the lease," his grandfather asked.

"Oh." He grabbed a jacket off the back of his room's folding chair and shoved one arm in. So much for all that work he'd done to keep the topic off his mind. Heck, he'd gotten so desperate for a distraction he'd sketched a silly scarecrow for Maddie, planned to leave it on her windshield when he walked out before her tonight. "I didn't."

"How long will they hold it for you?"

"Doesn't matter, Grandpa. I can't get that lease, not without opening my closet to show the whole town just how many skeletons are hiding in there."

He tried to ease past on his way to the door, but old Tom laid a hand upon his shoulder. "You can't spend the rest of your life avoiding all it has to offer just because of a few bad choices made in the past."

"Her bad choices, not mine."

Tom shrugged.

Cole stepped back. "Don't you get it? When news hits that you're harboring a convicted felon, life's just going to get messier for you, too. It could hurt your business, Grandpa. I won't do that to you."

"Rumors only hurt if you let them. Me, I'm too old to let gossip bother me. You don't like my store? Fine, drive twenty miles and find yourself another one."

Cole shook his head. Clearly, his grandfather didn't understand just how dark a shadow they'd both fall beneath if rumors of convictions and armed robbery made their way to Mount Pleasant. He'd spent all year making sure that didn't happen. Why risk it now?

"I know that look in your eyes, son. It's the same one your father used to give me when he was growing up. You may think I don't know what you're going through, but I do. More than you know.

"I didn't bring you up here to spend your life hiding away above my shop—I brought you up here to make a new life for yourself. Washing dishes and playing your guitar for Miss Ruby on Sundays is fine and dandy, but it's not how a man makes a good living. You're a man now, Cole. It's time to think like one. Make a name for yourself, start anew."

He felt his resolve begin to foolishly waver. Why did his grandfather always have to make so much sense? The man had never given him bad advice, so if there was anyone he could trust, it'd be him.

"But what if it fails? The shop, I mean. What if my reputation keeps it from even getting off the ground?"

Tom smiled. "Then you move on to the next idea, knowing you gave it your all. Because if I co-sign on this lease, young man, that's a promise you will make me—that you'll give it your all."

Cole looked around his grandfather's place, taking comfort in its warmth and familiarity. The old man didn't need much, didn't have much, but he always seemed to be content. What would it be like, to feel that way? To know exactly who you were and where you stood among your peers?

His gaze zeroed in on the dust motes, drifting lazily in a ray of light from the afternoon's setting sun. To subject himself to a background check would be like cutting a giant hole in his safety net of secrecy. Then again, it'd only be the real estate company who'd be the ones to see anything, right? And with his grandfather's name as primary contact, he might well be looked at as an afterthought.

"You sure about this? About risking your reputation on me?"

Old Tom met his wary gaze with a confident one of his own. "As sure as I was of bringing you here to begin with. You deserve more, Cole. Always did. I'll do whatever I can to help make that happen. Besides, it's a six-month lease. A relatively small risk with potentially big rewards, if you ask me."

He wrapped his grandfather in a gentle embrace, wishing he felt half as sure about the leap of faith they were about to make as the old man did. "Thanks, Grandpa."

"You're welcome, son." He patted Cole's back. "Now come on. You've got an application to fill out before you head to the inn."

"Application?" Cole glanced to his grandfather's cuckoo clock. "Thinking that's gonna have to wait until after my shift. Too many fields to fill out."

"Not if someone's already filled most of them in."

Cole felt his jaw drop. "You did? But how'd you know I'd say yes?"

Grinning, his grandfather turned for the door with a shrug. "Call it Granville intuition."

Chapter Nine

Maddie paced the Checkerberry's kitchen floor in a half panicked, half excited state. Tyson had turned up at the Quarter Clean-It this afternoon. And, stalker-ish or not, she'd turned up there shortly after he did. It'd been much busier today than the last time they'd gone, but as luck would have it, the sleeve-eating machine beside his was free. Careful not to get anywhere near the washer's undercarriage, she'd put her meager load of towels in and then angled for the seat beside him.

And just as Cole had predicted, her outfit caught his eye. Or maybe Tyson had just looked up because she momentarily blocked the sunlight he was using to help read his *Muscle Fit* magazine. Yeah, probably the latter. Regardless, he'd offered her a smile and hadn't run away screaming, so she'd taken that as a good sign. Better than good, actually, as they soon got to talking about jobs and food. And when he'd gone to leave, he smiled and said he'd see her around.

He'd see me around!

Was that a good sign? A brush-off? An open invitation

she'd missed for asking him out? Maddie needed Cole here and she needed him now.

Knowing it was pointless to stand there festering, she crossed the room and threw open one of her utensil drawers. Best to keep busy until she could interrogate him. Work had always been a surefire distraction from the stress of real life. Though, if she could just find her late grandmother's paring knife work could hurry up and get under way.

"Where is it?" she muttered, digging through the next drawer. And the next. "Dang it, Cole. Where'd you put it already?"

With a half growl she grabbed one of Ruby's old knives. It wasn't her favorite, but it'd have to do. Thankfully, it did the trick. By the time Cole walked in, she was elbow-deep in asparagus.

"Oh, there you are." She set her knife down and followed after him as he made his way to hang up his coat. What she really wanted to do was bombard him with the million and one "what do I make of my encounter with Tyson" questions. Instead, she tried to dial it back a few notches.

Okay, more like a hundred notches.

"Sooo. How was your afternoon?"

He gave her a wary look as he slipped out of his jacket. "It was all right. You?"

"OhmyGodIthoughtyou'dneverask."

She clamped a hand over her mouth. So much for playing it cool. His lips pulled into a half grin.

"I take it you saw Tyson?"

"Yes! And you were totally right—he looked right at me as I came over to sit by him." She cleared her throat, opting to leave out the part about blocking out the sun. "He asked how my arm was, apologized again for not being able to lift the machine up so we didn't have to ruin my sweater."

"We." Cole arched a brow.

"Yeah, you know. The three of us." She ignored his flat look. "Anyway, turns out he works at that new gym over by campus. And get this—we totally have something in common!"

"Wow, no kidding?"

"Yes! Well, sort of."

"Sort of?"

"Yeah. So, you know how I love to cook and experiment in the kitchen, right? Well, turns out he does, too. Only, where I'm creating four course meals, he's creating health smoothies."

"Oh sure, I can see how that's totally the same thing." He broke into a grin and headed for the sink.

"What? Cooking is cooking and eating is eating. So what if his meals fit through a straw?"

Cole's laughter rang out, and she couldn't help but cringe. Had that sounded as pathetic out loud as it did replaying in her head? Still, that Tyson was familiar with the kitchen made him an even better choice for asking to the gala. Now they'd have something to talk about when he was twirling her around the dance floor.

"Go ahead, yuck it up. But this is huge, Cole. Do you know how hard it is to find a guy who wants to have anything to do with a kitchen?"

"Nope, can't say that I do."

She reached out to bat him in the arm. "I'm trying to be serious here."

"Ouch! Fine, I'll be serious." He rubbed his upper arm. "So you caught his eye, you talked...did you get his digits?"

"His what?"

"His cell number, Maddie. Did you get his number?"

"No. Was I supposed to ask for it?"

"Depends how well it went, I guess. Or if he asked for yours."

"No, he didn't." She ran a hand over her hair. "Gah, I hate this! How am I supposed to know what to do or not to do? Is there a *Dating for Dummies* book out there or something?"

Cole turned and put a hand on each of her shoulders. "Stop stressing. This is supposed to be fun, exciting. Not like a root canal."

Maddie nodded. The warmth of his touch began to soothe her frayed nerves. Cole was right, of course. No sense in getting all cray-cray over a simple conversation.

Cray-cray—was that even a term people used anymore? She decided to keep that question to herself. No sense in coming off any more socially awkward that she already did.

Cole withdrew his hands and leaned back against the sink's edge. "So you two were talking, swapping…blender tales, and then what? His clothes finished and he just left?"

"No. I mean, we didn't talk the entire time. Just some of it. His dryer buzzed first, so he got up and started folding his darks. Just as he finished, my dryer buzzed. I got up to get it, and he smiled and said, 'See you around, Maddie.'"

"See you around." Cole nodded. "Definitely potential there."

"But what does that mean?"

"Uh, I think it means he'll see you—"

"Don't…say it." She ignored his teasing grin. "I mean… what do I do next?"

"My advice? Wear something that'll catch his eye again next time, and be ready to ask him out for coffee. Or a smoothie. You know, whichever you think he'd prefer."

Maddie threw him a dark look. "Oh sure, go ahead and laugh and we'll see just how long I keep you on after the gala comes and goes."

He faked a cough and turned for the sink. "You're the boss, boss."

"Darned right I am. Speaking of which—what'd you do

with my favorite paring knife, anyway?"

Cole went stock still. "What?"

"My paring knife. I used it Saturday, haven't seen it since you washed it. You didn't run off with it or anything, did you?"

An awkward moment of silence descended on the kitchen. Cole cast a dark look over his shoulder. "I didn't take anybody's knife."

"Sorry, I...it was a joke, Cole. I know you wouldn't take it."

He muttered something but kept his back to her. Fearing she'd unintentionally struck a nerve, Maddie left him be and went back to work. Her dishwasher remained distant the rest of the evening, and not until she slid a plate of slow-cooked rib tips his way after the dinner rush had ended did he marginally perk up. She made a mental note not to tease him about things coming up missing in the future.

Though, why a joke like that would bother him was a mystery to her.

...

Cole sat beside his grandfather in an overly potpourried office at Sheridan Realty the next morning, wishing Bob Sheridan would hurry it up already. The application had been approved, funding from the bank secured, and yet the aging small town bigwig seemed bent on prolonging their appointment. If he didn't know any better, it was to allow extra time to study Cole, now that his background check had been run.

Run and studied closely, judging by Mr. Sheridan's scrutinizing gaze. A change from the jolly welcome he'd offered Cole when he'd put down his deposit last week. Today, the older man looked like he was ready to spring from his leather wingback chair and rescue any of the gold-trimmed valuables on his desk if Cole so much as looked at them funny. And the glance Mr. Sheridan had exchanged with his receptionist when she'd led the Granvilles back to his office? Oh yeah, that not-so-subtle silent exchange had spoken volumes.

The proverbial closet door had officially been opened.

Cole frowned. All the work he'd done to crawl out from under that dark cloud, and what good had it done him? Not twenty-four hours had passed since filling out their joint application, and already an elephant had joined them in the room. What if he'd been wrong to listen to his grandfather? It was just a matter of time now before word got out. Soon no one would trust him.

No one, not even Maddie. And she'd already started to doubt him all on her own.

"I have to say, Tom, I was surprised to see your name as primary applicant on the lease." Mr. Sheridan steepled his hands beneath his chin, elbows perched on the arms of his chair.

"I can imagine—you know as well as I from our younger days at Holy Cross that I don't have a musical bone in my body. My grandson, though, he's got a God-given gift. I plan to see it get put to good use."

The look of superiority on Mr. Sheridan's face dimmed. "Indeed."

He picked up a set of keys from his desk and passed them to Old Tom. "The previous renter cleaned out the last of their things Monday, so you're free to use the place within the confines of our agreement. Six months is the term, to be paid each month whether you remain there or not. If you choose to extend your lease beyond that, you'll need to give me thirty days notice before the lease is up for a six-month extension. Though, if you get behind on your payments, an extension of the lease would be highly unlikely." His gaze shifted to Cole, the message clear. "Any questions?"

"No, sir."

"Very well, then. Good luck with your shop, gentlemen. And Tom, I'll be by later this week to talk vanities. Mama wants her bathroom updated before spring."

Cole's grandfather stood and reached to shake hands with his old hunting buddy. "Appreciate you working with us on this, Bob."

"Of course, Tom." Mr. Sheridan shook his hand, then gave Cole's a strong shake as well. "Cole."

"Mr. Sheridan."

Cole followed his grandfather out of the office, past the lobby, and out into the brisk October air. A cloudless sky blinded him, and he paused to let his vision adjust to the change in lighting.

"You did well, holding your tongue in there."

He cast his grandfather a scowl and started for their delivery truck parked in Sheridan Realty's small but neat and tidy lot. "That guy's as arrogant as the day is long."

"He's a businessman, Cole. Gotta make a living just like the rest of us."

"Well, he could make the same living without looking a country mile down his nose at clients if you ask me." Or judging people without knowing their whole story…

Old Tom shrugged and headed for the passenger side door.

"You don't want to drive, Grandpa?"

"Nah. Kinda like you driving me places. Makes me feel a bit like Miss Daisy."

Cole grinned as the two climbed in and fastened their seat belts. "Guess that makes me Hoke the chauffer, huh?"

"No." His grandfather held up the set of keys. "It makes you Cole Granville, CEO of Granville Guitars. Or whatever it is you plan on naming it."

Cole felt his heart wedge itself in his throat. No matter

the microscope Bob Sheridan had trapped him under the past hour, those keys represented freedom. His gateway to the American Dream, his chance to be somebody. And all because the man beside him, the one stable force in Cole's tumultuous existence, believed in him.

It was happening. It was really happening.

He took the keys and curled his fingers around them, knowing he'd remember that moment for the rest of his life. "Thanks, Grandpa."

"Don't thank me, son." Old Tom smiled. "Just work hard and make me proud."

Working hard wasn't anything new to him. The making proud part? Well, there hadn't been many opportunities to do that in the past. But he'd be darned if he wasn't going to do everything humanly possible to earn that designation. Question was, would the town keep an open mind once rumors started flying?

Cole glanced back to Sheridan Realty and saw the receptionist peering out at them from the mini blinds, phone receiver to her ear. Oh yeah, the rumor mill was definitely already at work. But who knew? Maybe the town would give him the benefit of the doubt. Maybe not. If his shop failed, though, it wouldn't be from his lack of trying.

He looked to his grandfather and offered him a nod. "I'll do my best."

Chapter Ten

Maddie peeked out from the kitchen's swinging double doors for the hundredth time Sunday, watching for Cole. He'd perked up after his Eeyore-like behavior on Wednesday, and for good reason—he'd found a way to get the lease on his shop downtown. He dove into renovations the minute he had its keys in hand, leaving him weary but jovial for his evening shifts at the inn. Though she worried he'd request to reduce his hours, so far he'd insisted the two jobs wouldn't conflict.

She hoped to heck he was right. Cole had quickly become a staple in her kitchen, always stepping up to help whenever she needed it and not once had he complained in the slightest. He was great at playing the role of guinea pig, too, helping taste test her seasoning of dishes or experimentations on new ones, and unafraid to give honest feedback. So far, she hadn't disagreed with any of his assessments. But above all, he was quickly becoming a trusted friend. Someone she felt comfortable to confide in about feelings and emotions—when she felt comfortable enough to voice them, that was.

And that scarecrow sketch he'd left for her the other day?

Well, that was about the best, silliest gift she'd received in a long while. Made her chuckle every time she saw it, now at home hanging on the side of her fridge.

Silly sketches aside, Maddie couldn't help but feel a sense of pride for her friend, knowing how huge it was to catch a break when chasing after your hopes and dreams. And though she still had gotten very little out of him on his history, he was starting to open up here and there to her.

From the sounds of it, he hadn't had a stellar childhood, either. Lots of relocating, little time to make new friends, doing tons of chores and odd jobs to help support his mom. It seemed odd to her that he referred to his mother as Daisy Mae. Though, the Masterson boys called their grandmother by her first name, so maybe it was just the way things worked in other families. But grandparents were different in her mind, sometimes adding in a first/last name to the mix to keep them straight. Most kids grew up with two sets, after all. Her Grandma Bea had been one of two for her, though the other had passed away when Maddie was fairly young. By then, Grandma Bea's name had stuck, and that's how it stayed.

This week, she'd thought of her often, wondering what Bea's take on Tyson would have been. Sure, he was friendly enough. Had a warm smile and killer physique. But there was something missing so far between them. There'd been no spark, no instant attraction. And while, yes, they'd exchanged digits yesterday afternoon thanks to Cole's coaching, and yes, he'd proposed via text this morning that they go out and grab a cup of coffee tomorrow between her lunch and dinner shifts, she didn't feel nearly as excited about it as she'd expected.

More like scared to death.

She paced the kitchen floor, re-checked her lunch roast for the dozenth time, then returned to the door. How long did it take people to move from the yard to the dining room, anyway? She'd snuck away before the closing prayer in anticipation of the smaller-than-usual crowd wanting a quick meal to warm them from the brisk October morn, but they seemed to be moving slower than molasses today.

To add to her irritation, she'd discovered another item missing from her kitchen—her favorite whisk, the one with the red handle that fit her hand perfectly. She swore she'd just used it a day or two ago, so unless it'd walked off on its own, it had to be in here somewhere. Maybe Cole knew where it was? Yet another reason she needed to track him down at lunch.

Voices sounded from the lobby, and she spied Brent and Kayla leading the way. No surprise there—Brent was an eating machine. Miles and Stephanie were close behind, followed by a few of this weekend's newest arrivals at the inn. Last came Ruby and Tom and…no Cole.

Maddie frowned. Maybe he'd had to use the restroom or something. He never turned down one of their Sunday lunches.

She headed out with baskets of rolls and butter, playing the part of chef and waitstaff as it was custom on Sundays to serve the meal family style, and angled for Tom's table first.

"A moving message as always, Mr. Granville." She offered him a polite smile. His messages had grown a bit longer lately, cutting a bit closer to the quick with all their talk of forgiveness and acceptance of those different from us. His prerogative, she guessed. "Did your grandson get lost on the way back in?"

Old Tom offered her a gracious smile. "Thank you, Madelyn. I'm afraid Cole won't be joining us for lunch today. He has a lot to do before the arrival of his first student tomorrow."

"Tomorrow?" She nearly dropped the breadbasket. "B-but he's not ready for customers yet, is he? If he opens his doors before the shop's fully set up it could hurt his business."

"Oh, the grand opening isn't set to happen for a few more

weeks. But one of the students he'd talked to a short while back saw him in there working and asked if he could get started right away." He leaned forward, a gleam in his eyes. "Seems he's trying to impress a lady friend, who's requested a serenade."

"So in other words, the guy lied and she called him out," Maddie said.

Mr. Granville shrugged, but Ruby chuckled at his side. "When the love bug bites, people are known to say and do the craziest things."

"All the more reason to wear bug repellant." Maddie frowned. "Knowing Cole, he'll work until he drops and probably didn't pack a single thing to eat."

"Why don't you take him some of our leftovers, dear, on your way home," said Ruby.

Maddie met her gaze, knowing darned well what the old innkeeper was up to. But she needed to talk to Cole, to get his advice on what to say and do on her coffee date tomorrow. Maybe bringing her relationship coach some sustenance would give him reason to shift gears from hard labor to soft skills training for a few minutes, anyway.

"You don't need me back in here tonight, correct?"

"No," Ruby said. "We've only a few guests until the bus tour group arrives tomorrow. Leave me a dinner suggestion on the refrigerator, something simple that serves eight to ten, and I'll see to that."

Maddie nodded and moved on, placing the remaining breadbaskets at even intervals the length of the long table. Cole wouldn't mind her stopping by with food, would he? No, she couldn't imagine him turning her away. That thought brought her an unexpected amount of relief. She needed to see him, to hear his words of reassurance about tomorrow's date, no matter how jokingly they were delivered.

Yes, that was why she needed to see him. For advice.

About Tyson. Not because she had trouble not thinking about Cole when he wasn't around. No, that couldn't be it. Only, the more she thought about it, the more worried she grew that her needing to see him was more likely her wanting to see him because she missed him when he was gone. And that idea scared her far more than any silly coffee date with Tyson.

Because Tyson was an experiment. But Cole?

Cole was real.

...

Cole straightened from the low shelf he'd just installed in his front window display, wiping sweat from his brow. At least he'd managed not to cut himself on this one. He learned the hard way with the other two sets that maybe reading the instructions wasn't such a bad idea after all and gained a new appreciation of the saying "blood, sweat, and tears." But he'd take his lumps and then some if it got him what he wanted most of all: his own shop, in his own community.

A place where he could finally belong.

He hated leaving the inn before getting a chance to talk to Maddie, though. She was always busy on Sunday mornings, between doing her work to feed the breakfast crowd and then preparing for an unknown number of diners at Ruby's open luncheons, but it never seemed to bother her. At those times, she was in her element—focused, intense. Today had been no different. She'd snuck in after he'd started playing before the service, and back out before his grandfather's closing prayer. And while he should have known to expect as much, not getting to talk to her before he left had him feeling unusually empty this afternoon.

Why, exactly, he wasn't sure. It wasn't like they were best friends or anything. Just a boss and her subordinate.

Bull, said a voice in the back of his mind. A voice he did his best to ignore. So what if he enjoyed her company? If he thought she was pretty and funny and smart and witty and…

Oh no.

Cole ran a hand through his hair. He could not allow himself to fall for the woman he'd promised to set up with someone else. Talk about masochistic—that'd be like volunteering to have your heart torn in two.

No, he needed to be smarter than that. Cautious. Besides, it was clear she didn't feel the same way. No, she'd lit up with excitement retelling him how his suggestions had helped her catch Tyson's eye in the laundromat earlier this week, and how the ball had kept rolling with an exchange of phone numbers when she saw him yesterday. The news brought color to her cheeks, and managed to dissolve the serious look she wore a bit too often. Clearly, Cole's coaching was working.

Yep, Tyson was going to be one lucky guy if he truly did have two brain cells in that muscle-minded head of his. A woman like Maddie wasn't for the weak of heart or spine, but Cole would bet anything she'd be committed and all in on any relationship, just like she was at the Checkerberry Inn.

He tried to picture it—him in a committed relationship. One that didn't involve moving every six months, or getting interrupted by family life. A future with a wife, maybe some rug rats eventually, and an honest-to-God home. A modest one, but with a sprawling lawn and large master bedroom, perfect for spending rainy days under covers, exploring curves, and lips, and…

Knocking sounded on the window before him, startling him out of his daydream. His gaze came into focus on a familiar pretty face, rosy from the cool air but adorned with a broad smile. Cole felt his own cheeks warm as Maddie held up what appeared to be a doggy bag from the inn. He hurried to the door and flipped the deadbolt.

"Sorry, ma'am," he said, not bothering to hide his natural

southern drawl, "but the store here's closed on Sundays."

She arched a brow, hand on her hip. "Well that's too bad, sugar, because I thought somebody could use a bit of food to stick to their ribs."

Sugar. Okay, her calling him pet names—terrible accent or not—wasn't going to help him keep his head on straight. He swallowed hard and tried to stay focused on playing the role of…well, what was his role today? It wasn't kitchen help. She must have heard from Tyson and needed some more dating advice. He rubbed the back of his neck and stepped aside to let her in.

"Food? Yeah, guess I'd forgotten about that."

"Of course you did. You're male and you're in 'go' mode. If I've seen it once, I've seen it a hundred times. Brent's notorious for it. Gotta force the issue to keep you all from getting hangry."

"Hangry?"

"You know, angry and grouchy because you're hungry? I know I get that way."

Cole grinned. "You don't say."

"Watch it, buddy—I haven't fed you yet."

"Good point."

Maddie set the bag down on a small folding table Cole had been using as a desk and looked around.

"Wow, Cole, things are really starting to take shape in here."

He gave the same space a skeptical look. Even after all the demolition and scrubbing and framing and painting he'd done, it still was nothing like what he envisioned. "You think?"

"Oh yeah. Looks a million times better than the shop in here before ever did." She smiled. "Your neighbors will be thrilled to have a classy tenant beside them."

I sure hope so. "Well, I've got a long ways to go yet. Hopefully they'll be patient with me. Some of the finishing touches will have to wait until lesson money starts coming in."

Maddie nodded, took a seat in one of the two small stools he'd bought to eventually go in the lesson rooms, and began unpacking the food she'd brought. Was that roast he smelled? Cole's mouth began to water. He set down his borrowed power driver and made for the table. *Tyson better love to eat, because his soon-to-be-girlfriend is a freaking miracle worker in the kitchen.*

"Speaking of which, your grandfather mentioned you had a student starting already tomorrow?"

"Yep. Wilson McCain tomorrow, and Sienna...something...on Tuesday."

"I heard about 'ole Will. How'd you find the other?"

Cole shrugged. "She heard me play at an open mic session on campus a few weeks back, said she was looking for a new instructor. I took down her name and number, said I'd reach out if and when the shop came to be. She seemed pretty excited about it when I called yesterday."

Maddie slid a plate in front of him then fished out a plastic fork and knife from the bag. "Oh, I bet she was."

"What's that supposed to mean?"

Maddie just shook her head and grinned. "If you don't know, I'm not gonna tell you, *Mr. Relationship Coach.*"

"You think she's taking lessons just to flirt with me?"

Maddie arched one brow.

"Oh, whatever," he said and dug into his meal. "Money's money, right?"

"Uh-huh. So how many other students jumped at the chance for a little one-on-one studio time with the soon-to-be-infamous Cole Granville, hmm? Surely Sierra wasn't the only one."

"Sienna. And is that jealousy I hear in your voice?"

Maddie's cheeks flushed a deep scarlet. "Don't flatter yourself, buddy. I'm just saying when a, well, someone who looks, and then calls... Oh, just trust me when I say she won't be the only one with boobs who signs up."

"Men have boobs, too, you know. I'll prove it, if you like."

"Good lord, keep your shirt on. I know darned well what men do and don't have."

Her cheeks darkened even more. Okay, so he probably shouldn't have said that. But he was riding high on hope and opportunities and in too good a mood to keep it bottled up. Besides, she was cute when disarmed, and Maddie disarmament didn't happen often.

"Well, if it makes you feel any better, my third student starts on Wednesday, and *his* name is Butch."

A smirk broke through the scowl on her face. "Butch?" She snickered. "Did you pick him up in a bar on campus, too?"

"Touché, touché." Cole popped a fork full of roast into his mouth and savored the way it melted on his tongue. He hadn't planned on working at the Checkerberry beyond this season, but if coming back in the spring would guarantee him a daily supply of Maddie's cooking, it might well be worth it. If he didn't tick her off one too many times between now and then, of course. "So, what really brought you by? Did he text you?"

"Oh. Yeah, actually he did."

The smirk faded into something much more...hesitant. Why did she do that, wield confidence like a sword in the kitchen but be timid as a mouse outside of it?

"And?"

She rubbed one arm up and down along the other. "Well, he kind of invited me out to coffee Tuesday. Between my lunch and dinner shifts."

Success! So why didn't he feel like giving her a high five? This is what she wanted, right? *Because it's not what you want*, whispered that pesky little voice again. He gave it a mental shove aside and did his best to look and sound happy for her.

"That's great! See? I told you if we got you two conversing

things would take off in no time."

"Easy for you to say, you don't have to sit there in some cramped coffee shop trying to think of non stupid-sounding things to say."

Cole chewed and swallowed his latest bite, shaking his head. "What? Since when do you struggle thinking of things to say?"

"Since always." She looked down.

"You never have that problem with me."

"Because you're…different."

Take that, Tyson. Maddie doesn't have to work to enjoy herself with me.

He shook his head, trying to get his mind back on track. *This is not about me, this is not about me…*

"Not like bad, different," she continued with a grimace. "Just, well, we work together. Have a common bond."

"And you and Tyson use the same fabric softener." He shrugged. She threw him a dark look. "Seriously, Madds, the guy is human, just like me, just like you. And he likes to cook or whatever. There's something you can definitely talk about."

"I guess so."

Her gaze shifted to her lap. Cole finished the rest of his meal and pushed the plate away, his protective instincts scratching at his subconscious. There was more to her worries, something from her past that'd scared her off. He felt a sudden desire to hunt down the bastard who'd hurt her, who'd stolen her smile. Now that would be something worth doing time for.

"What was his name, Maddie?" he asked softly.

She looked up. "Sorry?"

"His name. The guy that hurt you in the past."

"Oh. It wasn't like *that*, it just…" She shook her head and looked out the storefront window. After a long moment, she spoke again. "His name was Harrison. We, uh, went to culinary school together. He seemed like the perfect guy:

smart, handsome, and knowledgeable about the kitchen. When he chose the open spot next to me in a class, well, I thought I'd died and gone to heaven."

She grinned at a private joke, then offered him a fleeting glance before returning her gaze to the view of downtown. "See, growing up, I didn't have a lot of friends. My parents were gone for long periods of times overseas—entrepreneurs with no time for an unplanned kid—and my grandmother needed help in her bakery. So when I wasn't at school, I was helping her. And truly, I didn't mind—it's where my love for cooking began. But it wasn't so good for my social life.

"Harrison said he understood, his childhood had been rough, too. Said he needed to do well in school to keep his scholarship." She cast Cole a bitter smile. "He said a lot of things I wanted to hear. Unfortunately, naive me didn't realize it was all baloney until after he stole my original recipe at the end of the semester and walked away the class star."

Cole's hands balled into fists. It was a good thing he didn't know this jerk's last name. A very good thing. Texas justice wasn't the same as it was up here. That douchebag wouldn't know what'd hit him.

She barked a humorless laugh. "Yep, Fattie Maddie had been played like a fiddle and tossed aside the minute he aced his project."

"Don't. You're not fat."

"I'm not exactly skinny by today's standards, either. You know what he told me when I confronted him? When I called him everything but white in the parking lot that day?"

He didn't want to know, was afraid of what he might do if he heard. But she needed to get this off her chest, needed to vent. Hopefully, him listening would help. "No, what?"

"That he was glad the class was over, so he could go back to sleeping with women his preferred size." She shook her head. "I was a little heavier back then, but—"

"Stop right there. No woman should be talked to like that. Ever."

Maddie shrugged and Cole worked to keep his temper in check. He'd encountered enough men like this Harrison in his youth, men who had talked down to his mother. Slapped her around when she didn't say what they wanted to hear or do what they wanted her to do. Apparently bullies came in all shapes, sizes, and socio-economic classes after all.

Cole found his resolve to set Maddie up with Tyson renewed. She deserved to be with someone who made her happy. Made her feel valued, desired. And if that muscle-head didn't fit the bill, then Cole would find someone who would.

"Harrison was a complete and total idiot. If he couldn't see what an amazing woman you are both inside and out, then it's his loss, not yours. Though, for his sake? We'd better not cross paths in any dark alleys down the road." Her eyes widened and Cole regretted saying that last part aloud. "But none of that matters anymore. He's history, and you're moving on."

She blinked away whatever thought she'd gotten lost in. "I am?"

"Yep. In fact, I predict you're going to nail this coffee date Tuesday. Tyson will be wrapped around your little finger before either of you finish your drinks. Why, he'll be begging to go to the dance with you."

"The dance! Oh my gosh, it's in less than three weeks!"

"Time to step up our game, Maddie. And with my coaching, you can't go wrong."

"Thanks, Cole." She leaned over and wrapped her arms around him, her face turned from his as she rested her cheek on his shoulder. "You're the best."

He swallowed hard, slow to embrace her as his heart stuttered from the unexpected display of affection. She smelled of sweets and sunshine, her hair of flowers and flour.

And her body, though coming at him from an awkward angle, felt so right in his arms.

Oh yeah, he was a goner. Too bad she didn't feel the same way about him.

"Anytime, Maddie," he said, pulling her closer to savor the moment, fleeting as it may be. "Anytime."

Chapter Eleven

Maddie sat at a corner table in Ground Level, the low-calorie smoothie bar-slash-coffee shop a few blocks from the laundromat, watching Tyson at the counter as he placed their orders. She'd been a nervous wreck this morning, anxiety bringing on heartburn that could have scorched half the state. But a quart of Pepto and one encouraging text from Cole later and she'd not only pulled herself together, but managed to assemble a semi decent-looking outfit to boot. Now if only she could be as smooth the next hour as she'd practiced being in her mind.

Smooth like she was with Cole. Darn it, why did he make it so easy to just be herself?

Tyson glanced over, saw her watching him, and smiled. The resulting dimples softened his muscular physique, making him look far less intimidating than usual. She looked away with a sigh, still not quite believing a guy like that was here with her. *When I walk into the gala with Tyson in tow, Miles's jaw is gonna hit the floor.*

Now that thought spawned a broad smile. Maybe she

could have Cole there to videotape it, so she wouldn't miss a second of that reaction. Without him, after all, she'd not be anywhere near this close to making that moment happen. Hopefully the hug she'd sprung on him Sunday hadn't freaked him out. She still didn't know what had moved her to do it—heavens knew she wasn't a hugger. But that's what friends did to show their appreciation sometimes, wasn't it? An innocent hug?

Though, if she'd known he would smell so good—all sawdust and earthy cologne—she might have opted for a pat on the back.

And why on earth was she sitting here, on a date with Tyson, thinking about Cole?

"Did you see a new store is going in where that print shop used to be?"

Maddie honed in to the conversation between two college-aged girls a table over, relieved for the distraction. Clearly, she was in over-thinking mode again. She cast a subtle look over one shoulder to spy a tall brunette sitting across from a petite blonde.

"Yeah, but did you hear who's running it?" asked the blonde.

"No, who?"

"Remember the eye candy who walked up to open mic night at the Java Stop a few weeks back?" asked the blonde.

"Stone? Flynt? Dang it, what was his name?"

Cole, you twits.

"Cole," said blondie.

"Cole," the brunette echoed in a dreamy voice. "Cute *and* a bad boy. Makes me want to take up guitar just to get some one-on-one time with him in the back room."

Maddie gripped the edge of the table to keep from hauling off and hitting anyone. Cole was more than eye candy and definitely no playboy. At least, not that she knew of. Though, the more she thought about it, how much did she know about him?

"Wait, bad boy?" blondie asked.

"Yeah, rumor has it Sheridan almost didn't give him the lease"—the brunette lowered her voice as footsteps sounded nearby—"because *somebody* did time down in Texas. Grandpa dearest had to step in and vouch for him."

Did time? Cole? Didn't the people around here have anything better to do than sit around making stuff like that up?

Maddie spun in her seat, retort locked and loaded, and found Tyson towering over her, a smoothie in each hand. The smile he wore faded to a look of concern.

"If you wanted something else I can go back up and..."

"No! No, I'm sure whatever you ordered for me will be awesome. Just...there was a fly, is all," she lied, swatted at the imaginary pest, and offered the best smile she could muster. "I'm kinda neurotic when it comes to bugs near food."

He sat the drinks down with a chuckle and maneuvered into the seat across from her. Maddie breathed a sigh of relief. Today's date had to go well if she was going to be able to pop the question about the gala and leave him enough time to rent a tux. Better get her head in the game and stop thinking about Cole. Still, what those silly college girls had said about him bothered her.

He didn't really have a rap sheet...did he?

She tried to picture him committing a jail sentence-worthy crime and couldn't. He seemed like such an honest, hardworking guy. But maybe he wasn't always like that, whispered a small voice in the back of her mind. What if he'd been a drunk? Or violent?

No, she couldn't imagine it. He was anti-wine, and had never lashed out at her during one of her kitchen rants. But what about theft? Her kitchen tools were walking off with more frequency than ever before. Could it be she had a klepto in her midst?

"Okay, so I ordered me the number six," said Tyson. "Need to load up on protein and carbs before my cycling class this afternoon. For you I got the number two—it's mostly fruit, a bit on the sweeter side. If you don't like it, though, you're welcome to order something else. A coffee, even, if you'd prefer."

She met his gaze and felt a zing of guilt. He was being sweet and attentive to her needs, and here she sat, thinking about another guy. There was nothing she could do about Cole and the rumors she'd overheard right now. Probably, they were just stories made up by a jaded co-ed he'd not paid enough attention to after his performance at that Java place. So Maddie pushed her worries, and the unsettling feeling of cute, younger women hitting on her friend, aside to mull over later. Right now, Tyson was who she should be focusing on.

And locking in that date to the gala.

"Nah, I'm sure I'll love it." She drew the drink close and flashed him a coy smile. "So, tell me more about these smoothies…"

...

Cole watched his second student step out the shop's door, Sienna's hips swinging in a "keep watching, baby" kind of way, and breathed a sigh of relief. Okay, so maybe being a private tutor hadn't been as easy as he'd expected it to be. Wilson had been fine, but Sienna…oh, boy. She'd been far more interested in learning about Cole than the guitar in her hands, which totally confused him. Sienna had been so excited about the prospect of taking lessons the last time they'd talked, and then when they spoke on the phone. How was he to know she had ulterior motives?

Maybe it'd be a good idea to have the lesson room walls made of plexiglass, he thought, looking at the shop through wiser eyes. To keep everything on the up-and-up. And cameras in each, just to be safe.

He ran a hand through his hair. Yeah, he had a lot to learn about being a business owner, but one distracted lesson wasn't about to shake him loose from his dreams. There would be other students, other musicians looking for repairs or purchases. And as business grew, so would his offerings. For now, though, lessons and repairs would have to be his mainstay.

With a sigh, he turned to gather his cell and jacket. It was three o'clock—time to get cleaned up for his shift at the Checkerberry. Cole grinned. He could practically hear Maddie going off about Sienna's behavior already. Probably, she would tell him to drop the girl and move on, to avoid trouble.

The bell hanging over the shop's front door jingled and he cringed. *Please don't let it be Sienna back again...*

"Forgot something?" he asked, turning toward the door. But it wasn't Sienna who'd entered the building, it was Robert Sheridan. And he looked far less thrilled to see Cole than Sienna had. "Mr. Sheridan. Sorry, I thought you were a student of mine."

"I've no intention of taking music lessons from you, Mr. Granville."

Cole nodded, rather relieved to hear that confession. If he had to be in a small space with this much air of superiority for long he might well choke. Sheridan stepped farther into the shop, shrewd eyes taking in the room before him.

"I see. Was there something else you needed?" said Cole. "I assume you have a reason for your visit today."

"How has business been?" Mr. Sheridan asked, sidestepping his question as he perused the contents of a display case filled with string and pick samples.

"I won't technically open until the end of the month, sir. Lots of remodeling left to do. But I've started with private lessons ahead of time to bring revenue in."

"Mmm-hmm."

Mr. Sheridan nodded, his gaze passing over a specialty pick autographed by Eddie Van Halen. Clearly, he wasn't here to shop. Cole bit back a suggestion for the man to hurry up and leave already.

"You'll have my rent payment on time, sir, if that's what you're concerned about."

At that, the man did look up, his gaze locking with Cole's. "Good. Because if you're so much as an hour late, Granville, I'm revoking your lease. You see, the mayor's son apparently had his eye on this storefront as well. Unfortunately for him, you acted on it first. Unless, of course, you'd like to change your mind."

"No, sir, I wouldn't."

"A shame. Gavin would do a nice job with this place. Keep the riffraff out, unlike the kind you'll be bringing in."

Cole felt the hairs on the back of his neck rise. "Is that so?"

"I saw your background report, son. I know who you really are."

Cole could see in the man's eyes it was no use arguing with him—his mind was already made up. Why try to set the record straight with someone who obviously wouldn't listen? Instead he stood up taller and leaned slightly forward.

"Let's just say that what really happened and what that report you saw listed don't exactly match. And as it didn't prevent me from being approved for this lease, I'm going to again ask why you're here."

Sheridan's gaze narrowed. "It's a good thing your grandfather and I go a long way back, son."

"Yes," said a familiar voice from behind Cole. "It is."

He spun to find his grandfather there, a quiet fury brewing in his eyes.

"I came to pick you up," Old Tom said, answering his question yet unasked. "Knew you had a second job to get to."

"Yes, I do."

Mr. Sheridan spoke up. "You should have told me, Tom—"

His grandfather continued, ignoring Sheridan's comment. "Why don't you show Robert out and lock up, Cole. He's stayed beyond his welcome. I'll be in the truck waiting."

Cole nodded and stepped forward to usher Sheridan to the door.

"He won't always be here to bail you out, you know," the man said in a low voice as they approached the door. "I'll be watching you closely, son, waiting for you to mess up. And when you do, you'll regret ever coming to Mount Pleasant."

Cole pulled the front door open, gripping the door's handle so hard it hurt. Better that than punch the arrogant jerk in the face. "Thanks for stopping by Mr. Sheridan. Come again when you'd like to learn more about *guitars*."

Robert Sheridan strode out the door with a harrumph. Cole watched him go, glad to be rid of the man, and flipped the door's lock into place. Would it be like this the entire term of his lease, he wondered, or would the guy learn to lighten up?

Probably the first, not the latter. Though, if today's visit was meant to scare off Cole from his commitment, Sheridan had royally screwed up. Because rather than scare him, Cole was more determined than ever to make his business grow. With a shake of his head he grabbed his things and headed out the back door, locking it behind him. True to his word, his grandfather sat in the delivery truck's passenger seat.

"Thanks for the lift, Grandpa. But I think I could have

managed the two block walk home."

"Oh, I'm sure you could have. Though, from the sound of it, my timing couldn't have been better."

Cole turned over the ignition with a frown. "That guy's a real piece of work."

"Robert's heart isn't completely black. Mostly, maybe."

"Great." Cole chuckled. "Well, thanks for the heads-up."

"Anytime. Speaking of which, that's why I came by — to give you a heads-up."

He shifted into reverse and paused. "Oh? About what?"

"A few of my regulars stopped into the store today, asking if the rumors about you were true. Seems someone at Sheridan's office took it upon themselves to share what they saw in your background check."

"Dammit." Resentment washed over Cole anew. All these months he'd been so careful to keep his past buried, out of sight. He knew he shouldn't have listened to his grandfather. This co-signed lease had been a bad idea from the start. But how do you say no to the one person in this world who's looked out for you from day one?

Though, now he had a second person he'd like to think was looking out for him: Maddie. But what would she think when the rumors reached her ears? Would she be like Sheridan and the others, assuming the worst about him, or would she give him a chance to clear the air? The thought stung, more than it should.

Face it, you're falling for her.

He barked a soft, humorless laugh. A fine mess he'd gotten himself into. Then again, if his rap sheet scared her off like it had a habit of doing for everyone else, it'd soon be a nonissue.

But she wouldn't turn her back on him that easily, would she?

Only time would tell. In the meantime, he'd have to add "damage control" to his daily list of responsibilities.

Tom placed a gentle hand upon Cole's shoulder. "You can't live your life hiding from your past, son. You've got to own it and move on."

"Yeah, well, unfortunately, Grandpa? Sometimes that moving on part isn't completely up to just me."

"Give the town a chance, son."

"I'm trying, Grandpa," he said, looking out the windshield at the backside of his new shop. "Hope it'll give me one, too."

Chapter Twelve

Maddie walked out of the kitchen after breakfast Wednesday morning, mentally preparing her day's to-do list. She had a lot to work in between her lunch and dinner shifts, including getting the nerve up to ask Tyson if he'd like to come over for dinner on Friday. Their smoothie date had gone well. No fireworks yet, but well nonetheless. He was a nice guy, very pleasant, but did like to talk a lot about eating healthy. And being healthy. And how great being and eating healthy could be.

Yeah, so he might be on the verge of health-obsessed, but she could think of a hundred worse things he could be. Unfortunately, their date had been cut short by a call he'd gotten from work, asking him to come in early to cover another cycling class for an ill instructor. Which meant she still hadn't asked him to the gala yet.

When she bellyached about it to Cole last night, he'd suggested she invite Tyson over for dinner.

"Dinner? At my place?" The thought had nearly terrified her. "I don't think I'm ready for that quite yet. I mean, being alone with him, away from the crowd."

Rather than be the usual voice of reason she needed to hear, he'd just shrugged and gone back to his dishwashing in silence. Twice she'd asked later in the evening if everything was okay. Both times, he'd nodded and said it was nothing. Baloney. Something was eating at him, and if she had to bet she'd say it had something to do with that Sienna chick.

So on top of worrying about the gala, she was worried about Cole. And that bizarre rumor she'd heard yesterday. She'd wanted to ask him about it, to clear the air and probably have a good laugh about how ridiculous it was, but with the mood he was in she'd held back. Plus, they got crushed at dinner last night, that busload of tourists a hungry bunch, and the evening had flown by before she'd really had a chance. Next thing she knew, it was nine thirty and he was mumbling good-bye.

"Want me to walk you out?" she'd asked, hoping for a chance to talk outside.

"No," he'd said, not meeting her gaze. "Thanks anyway."

He'd left without another look back, which was unlike him. But when she came out to her car, he'd left another folded note on its windshield. Inside was another scarecrow sketch, only this one had been given wings. Beneath it were a few lines from a Journey song they'd heard on the radio in the kitchen that night. She'd sung along, trying to fill the void, but he'd remained quiet. Guess he'd been listening after all.

Maddie took the note from her pocket and ran a hand over the sketch, so simple and yet a million times better than she could ever do. He was so stinking talented. And thoughtful. No way could those silly rumors be true. With a sigh, she tucked it back in her pocket and headed for the lobby, hopeful he'd be in a far better mood tonight.

"Madds?" Miles popped his head out of Ruby's office. "You got a few minutes?"

Great. Rarely when Miles wanted to see her did their discussions ever take a few minutes. But what prompted this talk? She hadn't ordered anything all week.

"Yeah, all right. But only a few, I've got a lot to do."

"Ah." He grinned, stepping aside to allow her passage. "The new main squeeze keeping you busy, eh?"

"That is none of your business," she said, then drew to a stop as she found Ruby, Kayla, and Brent already seated in the office. "W-what's going on?"

"Someone stole from the cash register last night," said Miles, closing the door behind her. "Three hundred dollars."

Her gaze flashed from his to Ruby. "Really?"

"I'm afraid so. Unfortunately, from what the others have told me, this is not the first item to come up missing."

"No, it's not," said Kayla. "Brent had a few power tools go missing that he'd left in here on Friday, and the album with all those autographed pictures in it has been missing for several days now. We thought maybe one of the guests had taken it up to their room to look at it, but none of them seemed to know anything about it."

"Have you noticed anything missing in the kitchen lately?" said Brent.

Maddie swallowed hard. "Yes."

He arched a brow as she ran a hand over her hair, not liking where this was going. Because if she was reading them all right, it wasn't anyone in this room under suspicion, it was a certain new member of their staff. One she'd just discovered from the town's rumor mill may have a darker past than he'd let on before.

"I thought maybe at first they were just things that'd gotten misplaced after they'd been washed," she said. "Totally understandable, when you're training a new person in the kitchen. But I've torn the place apart and not found a single one. The weirdest part is they're mostly antique items, things my grandmother handed down to me. They've got more sentimental value than anything." She looked to the others. "Surely, you don't think Cole—"

"We don't want to think that way, but the timing does seem a bit coincidental, don't you think?" said Miles.

Maddie planted a hand on each hip. "Oh, sure. Blame the new guy. But I'm telling you, he didn't do it."

"Are you willing to bet your next paycheck on that?" he asked.

"Miles, please," said Ruby. "The Granvilles are good friends of this family, and I can hardly imagine Tom not knowing he had a thief living under his own roof. Besides, Maddie has worked closely with him for several weeks now. If she believes him innocent, then I am partial to her opinion over that of rumors flying around town."

"So you heard them, too," asked Maddie.

Ruby frowned. "If there's one thing this town loves, it's a scandal. Unfortunately, that means if we call and report these thefts to the police, we'll only fuel the fire."

"What do you suggest we do, Grandma?" Brent asked. "We can't just sit back and do nothing."

"No," said Kayla, a thoughtful look on her face. "But we might be able to hold off involving the police if we do some surveillance of our own. Lots of places have security cameras mounted near cash registers and valuables. And I know they sell wireless ones that we could probably set up here fairly easily without spending a fortune. If you'd like, I can do some research, get some quotes on how much it might cost."

Miles nodded. "Probably not a bad idea, especially if business continues to improve."

"If worse comes to worse, we could always look into having a private company do the work," said Brent. "Cameras, monitors, alarms. Keeps us out of having to mess with it."

"No offense, cuz, but I'm hoping Kay finds us a cheap and

easy alternative. I looked into those private companies a few years back. Would cost us an arm and a leg."

"Spoken like a true penny-pincher," said Brent.

His cousin scratched an imaginary itch on his forehead with a middle finger. "Says the guy who's needing power tools replaced."

Brent gave Kayla's knee a light smack. "You heard the man, sweetheart. Go find us a deal."

They all laughed and prepared to disband. Miles, however, caught Maddie's arm and held her back.

"Look, I know you believe he's innocent, but I think until we know for sure what's going on it'd be best to keep an eye on Cole as he's coming and going. At least until we get this surveillance gear set up. You cool with that?"

She wanted to say no, that she was most certainly not okay with that. But like it or not, the overheard conversation in the cafe yesterday had planted a kernel of doubt in her mind. A kernel that, until someone shined a light on his true background, was getting harder to ignore. So rather than pitch the fit she should have pitched, Maddie gave Miles a small nod.

"That's my girl. And, Madds?" he said as she turned to go.

"Yeah, Miles?"

He met her gaze, sincerity clear in his eyes. "I hope you're right about Cole. Anyone who can get you laughing like he does in the kitchen oughtta be a keeper."

...

Cole finished the last of Maddie's dishes Tuesday, his mind racing just as much as it had been when he'd walked into the Checkerberry that night. Usually between the hot soapy water, the mindless repetition, and Maddie's snarky humor, a shift at the inn was like a healing salve to his soul. But with his past reemerging and doing its darnedest to bite his future in the rear, nothing seemed to be working.

"You about done over there?"

He pulled the drain stopper and turned to find Maddie stripping off her apron. Which stank, as he wasn't looking forward to heading home where he was sure to fester for another hour or two until sleep finally pulled him under. "You in a hurry tonight?"

"Nah, just been a long day."

Tell me about it. His lesson with Sam, a sophomore over at Central Michigan who, thankfully, was far more interested in the guitar than Sienna had been, went swimmingly. But arriving at the shop to find someone had egged the front window and left him a nastygram on the back door—"*We don't need your kind ruining our town*"—had left him far too unsettled to enjoy that small victory.

Again, he felt frustration toward his grandfather. And again, he pushed it aside. If Old Tom said it was best to move on then he had to trust him. Too bad it looked like the town might be planning on dragging him through hell and back along the way.

He gathered his things and joined Maddie at the swinging double doors. "This feels…different."

"Yeah." She shrugged. "I'm a workaholic. So sue me."

"Then good for you for taking this first step toward recovery," he said with a wink. "Or is there a hot date with Tyson planned for tonight and you're just trying to be discrete around the others?"

"No. And thanks."

Okay, something was up, he just didn't know what. A quick glance at his boss found her walking faster than normal. And…tense.

"What's going on?"

She looked to him in surprise. "Nothing. It's just…I'm…

nervous. About my dinner date on Friday. Ruby gave me the night off, so I asked. He said yes."

Ah, there it was. Silly girl. When was she going to believe him when he said she had nothing to worry about? Tyson was one lucky guy, even if his date had yet to see it. He held the back door open and followed her out into the still, chilly night. A full moon loomed overhead, making the inn's emptied swimming pool practically glow.

"Okay then, dish. What's got you so worried it's driving you from work?"

Her shoulders sank. "Look, it's no big deal. Just…I'll be fine."

Complete denial. Cole followed her to her car and stepped in front of the driver's side door before she could slink away. "You'll feel better if you talk about it."

"Right." She cast him a dark look. "Because I haven't told you nearly enough about my insecurities already. Why not add more to the pile?"

He smirked but didn't say a word. Crossed his arms. Leaned back against the car.

"Oh, all right!" She balled her hands into fists. "I'm scared, okay?"

"Scared? Of Tyson?" He'd hunt down the guy if he so much as harmed a hair on Maddie's head, size difference be damned.

"No. And yes." She ran a hand over her head. "I…I haven't been physical with a guy in a long time. Like, long, long time. And I'm worried I'll screw it all up."

Physical. As in… Cole swallowed hard. He shouldn't be chasing those images, but now that she'd hinted at them, they were clawing at his imagination. Her hug the other day had already sparked daydreams it shouldn't have, her continued kindness amid a town of doubters only fueling the fire.

"Oh, Madd—"

"Don't. Don't give me that 'Oh, Maddie' crap. People like you walk around the planet not having to worry about stuff like this. Girlfriends for you have probably been a dime a dozen. Maybe cheaper."

She thought he was a catch? Cole filed that tidbit away for another time, another daydream. Right now, she needed her confidence built back up. "You're not giving yourself enough credit."

"Whatever. My track record says otherwise."

He shrugged. "A lot of guys are intimidated by smart, confident women."

"A lot of them also aren't attracted to women who aren't built like a twig."

"What's it going to take for you to understand that most guys I know would pick a curvaceous body over a twig any day?"

"Right, which is why women like me are plastered all over the covers of Cosmo and GQ, huh?"

"Those magazines target women who are insecure about the way they look. Hell, half the women featured have been Photoshopped beyond recognition." Cole worked to contain his frustration. Her last boyfriend really had done a serious number on her. "And what are you looking at those stupid magazines for anyway?"

Her chin jutted out, stubborn as ever. "I was looking for some tips, if you absolutely have to know."

"Tips?" He laughed. "What, I'm not doing a good enough job as your dating coach?"

The confidence in her eyes faded as quickly as it'd arisen, and she started toeing the gravel at her feet. "It's not that. This, well, I was looking for tips on a topic I didn't think it'd be fair to ask you about. Since you're a guy and all."

"Nice that you noticed." He threw her a grin, but she was still staring at her feet. God, he wanted to make her feel better. Make her understand just how amazing she was. How amazing he knew her to be. "Madds?"

"Yeah?"

She looked up, vulnerability clear in her eyes, and he knew what he had to do even if he'd pay for it in the quiet of his room later. Cole took a step forward. "What you're looking for isn't in those magazines. It's experience. And watching for the signs."

He shifted his gaze to her lips. So full and perfect, parted slightly in surprise.

"T-the signs?"

"Yeah. Like where he's looking. Or if he moves closer."

Cole closed the distance between them and raised a hand to cup her chin. Her eyes widened a fraction but she stood stock-still, like a doe in headlights.

"So, I shouldn't punch him if he does this?" she asked, the sound barely above a whisper.

"Definitely not."

He lowered his face to hers, allowing his own eyes to drift shut only after hers did first, and brushed his lips lightly over hers. They felt as soft as they looked, like velvet. So tempting, so very tempting. God, he wanted to kiss her. Kiss her until they both forgot their names, their troubles. But she wasn't his, much as he hated to remind himself of that.

She raised her hands to his chest, and Cole feared she might push him away. But she didn't, hallelujah, allowing him to savor her touch a bit longer. To explore without completely overstepping the boundaries. He slipped a hand to the small of her back. Kissed one corner of her lips. Brushed his lips across hers to kiss the other. So very soft…and so *not* his.

He skimmed her cheek with his lips, pressed a kiss to the hollow beneath her ear. A stray hair ticked his nose, teasing him. Oh, how he wished her hair wasn't pinned back so that he could run his fingers through it. He knew from that hug on

Sunday it felt as silky as it looked.

"Cole?" she whispered.

Reluctantly, he drew back. God, she looked beautiful, her skin awash in the pale moonlight. "Yes, Maddie?"

"Will you kiss me already?"

Permission. His smile widened. "Yes, ma'am."

And so he did. Sweetly at first, barely any pressure at all. She leaned into him, tentative, kissing him back. When her mouth opened he followed suit, allowing her to explore with her tongue and him doing the same.

This kind of coaching he could do all day. It was pure heaven, even if he was behaving more like a little devil, stealing kisses from the girl he'd promised to set up with another man. The selfish part of him wished this moment would never end.

He should have known better, of course—Cole never had that kind of luck. No sooner had the thought entered his mind than a car's keyless entry *bloop-blooped* a few spaces over from them. Maddie drew back, lips swollen but curved into a sheepish smile. To their left, a couple strode down the inn's back walk, pretending to ignore them but each wearing the same, knowing grin.

"I, uh, guess I should be going," she whispered. "Before Ruby fires me for PDA on the clock."

"You know, technically you're not on the clock anymore. And I can't say I've ever heard of someone being fired for kissing a scarecrow."

"Oh. Well, in that case," she pressed one last kiss to his lips, then raised up on tiptoes and whispered in his ear. "Thanks for the lesson, Coach."

"Anytime." He stepped back from the car, not wanting her to go but not wanting her to know that, either. For her, it was training. For him? Pure Heaven. And darn it if he wasn't left wanting so much more. "Practice makes perfect, you know."

Okay, so that last bit had slipped out. Cole mentally cringed at how pathetic he'd sounded. But instead of dishing out a snarky retort, Maddie flashed him a vibrant smile as she reached for her door handle.

"I'll keep that in mind."

He watched her go, adrenaline pumping through him, and prayed she would. And while all this was disguised as him coaching her for the big party with Tyson, Cole couldn't help but admit that a not-so-small part of him was beginning to hope muscle boy wouldn't stick around for long, so he could swoop in and have Maddie all to himself.

If, that was, she'd let him. Her kiss tonight hinted maybe she would.

And that spark of hope was the best thing he'd felt in a long, long time.

Chapter Thirteen

Maddie stood in her own kitchen Friday night, fanning herself while fighting the urge to run. A twentieth look at the clock found it to be three minutes after six. Tyson would be there any time now, which she should be thrilled about. Only, she wasn't, not after that kiss.

Her gaze instinctively drifted to the scarecrow, hanging on the side of her fridge.

Curse you, Cole Granville. You've ruined me.

His coaching performance had proved to be the best kiss of her life. So sweet, so giving...so downright stupid. What the heck had she been thinking, letting him kiss her like that? She fanned harder, ignoring the voice in the back of her mind reminding her that she'd kissed him back. Repeatedly. How could she not, when it'd felt so right?

Because it wasn't, replied her conscience. With a growl, Maddie tossed the paper fan onto the counter and checked her roast in the oven. Enough with the lamenting. And why bother? It was just a practice session. Cole'd probably kissed a hundred girls over the years. Why would he feel anything toward her after she'd driven away?

Deep down, she wanted to believe he had felt something. That there was a gentleness he'd offered the other night that he hadn't had to, a kindness in his eyes. And it hadn't been pity—she would have punched him if he'd looked at her like that on his approach. But his touch, his boldness, it'd disarmed her.

And now she was left to pick up the pieces. Stellar.

She'd just confirmed with the meat thermometer that the roast was in fact done when a knock sounded at the door. Maddie straightened, checked her reflection on the toaster, and headed for the door. At least tonight she hadn't had to worry about upsetting Cole with a pre-dinner glass of wine, because heck yeah there'd been one. Otherwise, she'd be so tightly wound that knock on the door might have sent her into the ceiling.

One giant heave-ho and the front door was open. On her stoop stood Tyson, a bouquet of fall mums in hand. Always so thoughtful. And yet even now, her mind kept reverting to Cole's kiss.

She wanted to cry and kick herself all at the same time.

Instead, she plastered a welcoming smile on her face, thanked him for the flowers, and ushered him inside. There was a meal to eat and a gala to attend. And maybe, if she'd stop being the world's worst person and give the guy she'd lured here a chance, she might actually enjoy herself.

• • •

"Must be kinda weird tonight, without Maddie here, huh?"

Cole looked up from his sink half full of dirty dishes and offered Kayla as good a smile as he could muster. "Yeah. Definitely a bit more…mellow."

"Just a bit."

She laughed and went back to chopping vegetables, humming as she worked. It struck Cole as odd that the sound was actually in tune—something that never happened when Maddie tried to do the same. And as much as it'd grated on him the first few days, he found himself missing the off-tune sound.

Missing her.

Okay, so maybe kissing Maddie hadn't been the wisest thing he could have done. But darn it, she'd needed a confidence boost, a pick-me-up. The tint to her cheeks and coy smile she'd left with said he'd accomplished that and more. Unfortunately, the hours and days after for him had become more and more difficult. Because while he'd claimed to be offering her kissing practice, the truth was he'd wanted to kiss her the day he started at the Checkerberry.

Nope, even that wasn't quite true. He'd wanted a taste of those lips the first time he saw her, this spring after playing his first Sunday service here. She'd set a breadbasket on the table before him and offered a warm smile. Only months later did he realize how rare that smile was freely given by the endearingly snarky chef. What had prompted him to be on the receiving end of her good graces that day he may never know, only that it'd been the start of a silly crush.

When she'd called after him that night in the driveway, asking if he would help her in the kitchen, he'd nearly told her no just to keep his distance. Because a girl like her deserved to be with a good, wholesome guy, not some southern screw-up.

"…and then I said, 'oh, yeah, I know the guy running it. You should totally go in and take some lessons.' So if a tall, skinny guy that looks a teeny bit like me comes in, that's my brother TJ."

Crap, he'd missed half the conversation. *Stop daydreaming about your boss, dumbass.* "TJ you said? Nope, haven't met him yet."

"Then I'll tell him to hurry up and get over there. Your slots are gonna fill up if he waits too long."

"I don't know about that," he said. "Business isn't quite what I'd hoped it would be."

She shrugged. "Give it time. Oh—do you have a website? That could really help kickstart it, especially if you're targeting the younger crowd. Heck, for them, if you don't have a website or an app, they might walk right by and not even look up from their cell phones to see it."

"Ah no. Not yet. Good idea, though."

A website. Right, like he had the money for that. Heck, the way lessons and his three measly string orders had been, he might not have enough to pay his lease this month. And wouldn't Robert Sheridan be pleased as a hog in slop if that happened…

"Well if you need help, let me know. Marketing's kinda my thing. Feel free to pick my brain any time."

Cole thanked her and turned back to his dishes, thinking about how lucky a guy Brent was. Kayla seemed like a real doll, always smiling and pitching in to help. Maybe if business picked up and he had a little extra revenue coming in soon, he'd take her up on the website offer. Couldn't hurt, that's for sure.

"So how is it, living with your grandfather and all?" she asked. "Is his place pretty big over the hardware store?"

"It's all right, I guess. Free room and board in exchange for chores and helping at his store, so I really can't complain. Keep telling him once I've got my shop up and running that I'll find a place of my own, but he insists he doesn't mind having me around." Cole grinned. "I think he gets kinda lonely."

Kayla leaned his way and lowered her voice. "Well if you ask me, I think Ruby's sweet on him. And from the way his eyes light up each Sunday when he takes his place next to her at the table, I'm thinking the feeling's mutual."

"Really?"

"You've never noticed?"

"Uh…" He thought back and tried to picture it but couldn't. Then again, usually on Sundays he was too busy thinking about his shop. Or watching for Maddie…

"Men." Kayla shook her head. "You guys wouldn't know love unless it hit you square in the face."

Cole chuckled. "Easy now, I resemble that remark."

"Which part? About being a guy, or being oblivious?"

"Well the first for sure."

"And the second?" Kayla arched a brow.

She sure asked a lot more questions than Maddie did. Cole shifted beneath the weight of her stare. "I don't know that I'd call myself oblivious. More like…realistic."

"Oooh, someone's caught Granville's eye," she murmured in a singsong voice. "Anyone I know?"

His jaw dropped open. Okay, so apparently Maddie had spoiled him rotten in the "do not pry" category. Kayla, however, was an entirely different breed of woman.

"Oh, quit your fretting, I was just messing with you. Heck, outside this building, I only know a handful of people, you and your grandfather included." She shook her head with a grin. "Though, judging by that look on your face, I'd say whoever it is she's got you falling hard."

He snapped his jaw shut. Hell yeah, she did. Too bad she wasn't exactly on the market, all thanks to him and his stupid coaching. "I don't know if I'd go that far."

"Uh-huh."

Lord, the woman was starting to make him nervous as a cat in a room full of rocking chairs. So much for her seeming all sweet and innocent. Cole gained a whole new appreciation for Brent in that moment. "Well it doesn't matter, because she's not in to me, so…"

"Why do you think that?"

Because I've been coaching her on how to win over another man. "She's kinda already seeing somebody."

"Oh," she said, a knowing look on her face.

Knowing? Oh no. Was she a mind reader, too?

"Kayla…"

"Hey, your secret's safe with me. I promise." She returned her focus to the cutting board. "Besides, I think it's kinda cute."

Cole dragged a hand across his face with a groan. "Is it that obvious?"

"Nah. I'm just good at reading people."

"Well stop reading, because this isn't happening."

"We'll see." She smirked.

He shook his head and turned back to the dishes, trying to block the hope rising in his chest. He'd come to Mount Pleasant looking for a do-over in life. To blend in with the scenery, grow some roots. Maybe fall in love. Memories of that kiss blossomed fresh in his mind.

But those memories were followed by images of eggings and glares and rumors and worry. What was he thinking, getting close to Maddie? He was a pariah, a disease. The longer he stayed in town now, the messier things were likely to get. And he couldn't do that to Maddie, couldn't jeopardize her reputation, her career. It didn't matter how badly he was falling for her, he wouldn't allow himself to be that selfish.

Besides, what would she do if and when she did find out the truth about his past? Would she still want him around? Still want him as a coach or even a friend? Not likely, not someone as grounded as her.

We'll see.

No, Cole told himself as he grabbed a dirtied pan from the sink's soapy depths. *For Maddie's sake, we shouldn't.*

Chapter Fourteen

Maddie had no sooner stepped foot in the Checkerberry's kitchen Saturday morning before being pounced on by Miles.

"So, how'd the date go?"

"What the—?" She whirled around, ticked at being startled at such an early hour. He sat on a bar stool next to the island kitchen, coffee mug in hand and thoroughly nonplused. If his eyes weren't so bloodshot, she might well have cracked a rolling pin over his head. "Don't you ever sleep anymore?"

"Steph's got a cold. She's snoring loud enough to wake the dead."

"You scare me like that again, and you'll be one of them."

Miles chuckled. "Tell you what—you trade places with me and see if you still feel the same way."

"Oh, whatever. You have the woman of your dreams sawing logs in that bed of yours. I've got crickets and noise from the street below."

He took another sip and watched her from over the brim of his mug. "So, I take it the date was a bust then?"

Maddie snorted and crossed the room to grab an apron…

and to put some space between her and Miles. Her temper was short enough as it was with men in general this morning. "Is meddling a gene in the Masterson family, or did you and your cousin just win the lottery on it? And how did you know I had a date, anyway?"

"Lucky guess, since Kayla was in here covering for you. On a Friday night." He winked. "And what did Brent do to piss you off, anyway?"

"He sent me a text at midnight, said if I needed to *sleep in*, he and Kayla would cover my shift."

Miles frowned. "And that's a bad thing?"

"It is when your date's long gone and you're already in bed fast asleep."

"Oh. Yikes. Totally bombed."

Maddie pinched the bridge of her nose. "Can't you go and pester someone else?"

"Nope." Miles took a long slurp from his coffee. "You're the only one awake at this hour."

"Lucky me."

She turned from him and flicked the oven on, then drew two trays of pre-made turnovers from the refrigerator. Technically, she could have come in a little later this morning, with breakfast already prepped and ready to go. But she couldn't stand the silence, the lingering scent of Tyson's cologne…

"Wanna talk about it?"

Maddie shot Miles a dark look. "Do I have a choice?"

He shrugged and took another drink from his coffee, clearly in no hurry to leave her be. She grabbed herself a cup of joe and leaned back against the counter across from him, letting the mug's warmth seep into her hands.

"I had him over for dinner."

"Who?"

Maddie frowned. "Tyson, the guy I met at the laundromat.

Sorry, I figured Steph had filled you in by now."

"She had. I just wanted to hear you say it." Miles smiled like the Cheshire cat.

"Watch it, Masterson. You're already on thin ice as it is today."

He held up one hand in surrender. "Go on."

"Anyway, we just never…clicked, you know? I was distracted, he was distracted." She shrugged, feigning indifference. "When he got a call from work and bowed out early—*again*—I honestly wasn't all that bummed to see him go."

"And this is the guy you're bringing to the gala?"

Crap. She'd already told Miles she had a date for the crazy prom thing. She took an unneeded sip of coffee to give her time to think. Lies, lies, and more lies.

Like how she kept telling herself that kiss between her and Cole was just practice and meant nothing…

"Yeah. At least, I hope he's still coming. He keeps cutting our dates short for work and I may kick him to the curb."

Okay, so that lie was a doozie. Not only was he not coming, she still had yet to ask him. But what Miles didn't know couldn't hurt him.

"Well, that pretty much sucks. Want me to knock some sense into him?"

At that Maddie laughed, long and hard. Miles's eyes narrowed.

"I'm glad I amuse you."

"Sorry," she said, wiping a tear from her eye. "It's just, well, the guy's built like a brick house."

"Bet I could still take him down," he muttered into his mug.

"You're right, buddy, you probably could…if you bored him to death with balance sheets and market trends."

"I come in here to cheer you up, and this is the thanks I

get?"

Maddie leveled him a look that said he wasn't fooling anyone. "You already admitted you're here because your woman snored you right out of bed. And from the looks of it, that coffee isn't doing you much good. Why don't you go crash in the Bourbon Room for a few hours, get some shut eye?"

Miles ran a hand through his stylishly unkempt hair. "Yeah, maybe I should. We've got a meeting with the FITS board later to finalize a few last-minute items for the gala. You sure you're all right?"

No longer feeling all that attracted to the man she's supposed to be dating, and feeling all sorts of attracted to the man she's not? Oh sure, she was feeling dandy.

"This is me we're talking about. Of course I'll be fine."

Miles studied her a minute longer, then shrugged in defeat. "If you say so. I'm too tired to argue any longer."

He rose from his seat and took his mug to the sink.

"Hey, that reminds me," he said. "Anything new go missing?"

"No, not since our little powwow the other day in Ruby's office. Kayla get the cameras up yet?"

"Yep," said Miles as he passed her on the way to the door. "Tested it out on parking lot surveillance that same night. Worked like a charm."

Maddie felt the blood drain from her face. Of course he knew about her and Cole kissing in the lot—Miles knew darned near everything that went on around here. Sure would have been nice to know the cameras were already in and working. Darn it! And here she'd been, feeding him lies and thinking he was actually buying them.

I guess the joke's on me this morning.

"Tell Cole I said hello when he comes in tonight, won't you? And while you're at it, ask him where he's put all your stuff."

She glanced up long enough to catch Miles's wink and flipped him the bird. Not that it fazed him in the least. He continued out the swinging doors without another look back, leaving her all hot and bothered, mentally reliving her kissing tutorial in the parking lot. The only thing keeping her semi-rational was Miles's last comment. Because Cole hadn't taken her things, and definitely wouldn't have taken any money from Ruby.

He was a good man, always so thoughtful. No way would he do that to them. Unless...

She pinched the bridge of her nose again, this time harder. No, she couldn't keep assuming every man that got close to her was only doing so to use her for something. Like Harrison had. That twerp had pulled the wool over her eyes all semester, but she'd sworn to never let herself be fooled like that again.

Cole was no Harrison, she knew it in her gut. But how to prove it to the others? To herself?

As she looked at tomorrow's dinner menu, though, a plan began to form in her mind...

...

Cole stood outside his shop midmorning Saturday, sponge and pail full of soapy water in tow. At first the eggings had seemed like harmless, random acts. But scrubbing crusty yolks and slimy egg whites off the window each morning was getting real old, real quick. When he'd broken down and called to report the vandalism yesterday, the desk sergeant had completely blown him off.

"It's just some neighborhood kids," he'd said. "Unless they damage something, there's not much we can do."

He thought that statement odd, seeing as when Cole was working in the shop a police cruiser drove slowly past on the hour every hour. Apparently he posed a greater threat than the town's egg throwers.

Damn rumors. It was just a matter of time before word on the street reached the Checkerberry, if it hadn't made it there by now already…

"Tough crowd, huh?"

Cole looked up from his work to find a guy about his age standing nearby, a lit cigarette in one hand and the other jammed into the pocket of a denim jacket. His hair was a rat's nest, and he was wearing shades dark as night. Still, he looked vaguely familiar. "Yeah. Guess not everyone's a music lover."

"Nah, it's probably the same little bastards who harassed the last tenant the entire time he was here. They've got nothing better to do than make everyone else miserable."

"You sound like you know a thing or two about the neighborhood," said Cole, rising to his full height.

The stranger shrugged. "Hard not to, when daddy dearest comes home rambling on about it after work every day."

Daddy dearest? "Guess so." Cole stepped forward and offered the guy his dry hand. "Cole Granville, by the way."

"Gavin McBride."

McBride, as in Leonard McBride, Mount Pleasant's long-standing mayor and another of his grandfather's old buddies. Which meant this was the guy who Sheridan had said wanted to rent the shop. Funny, he didn't look like the model son of a well-respected mayor.

"I had my eye on this place." Gavin paused to take a drag from his cigarette, then exhaled to the side. "Was thinking of opening a music studio myself. Guess you beat me to it."

Cole nodded, trying to keep cool. He couldn't tell if the guy was here to bully him out of the lease or just to make small talk. For now, he'd give him the benefit of the doubt. "You play?"

"Guitar? Hell no." His smile widened. "I'm a drummer."

Cole's memory finally slipped into place. "Ah, that's why you looked familiar. I saw you and your band a while back over near campus. You guys rocked it out."

"We do all right. Short a guitarist at the moment, though. Guy who's filling in isn't cutting it. If you know anyone who'd be interested, let me know."

He waggled his brows, then pulled a business card from his jacket pocket and handed it to Cole. Radar Love was the band's name, printed in big golden letters on a glossy black background. On the back of the card was Gavin's name and a phone number for lesson inquiries.

"You teach?" Cole asked.

"I give some lessons. CMU is teeming with rock-star wannabes, so I'm happy to take their money."

Cole snorted. "Yeah, well, they must all be gunning for drum lessons, 'cause it's been slim pickins for guitar students lately."

"Nah," Gavin said. "They'll turn up. Just gotta give it time." He rolled the cigarette's cherry off the end then toed it out on the sidewalk. "See you around, Granville."

"See ya."

Cole stared down at the business card still in his hand. Maybe he didn't need to spend money on a website or radio ads to draw attention. Maybe all he needed was a little time in front of the crowd and a few business cards of his own. Would gigging with McBride help ease him into the town's inner circle?

He pocketed the card and resumed his scrubbing, if nothing else relieved to have something to take his mind off the boss he couldn't have and his looming rent payment.

Chapter Fifteen

Maddie put the last of Monday's breakfast preparations away Sunday night, threw her apron in the laundry hamper, and went to collect her things. Cole had been more distant than usual the past two days, his smile not quite reaching his eyes. He looked tired, too, though whether from an oncoming cold or simple exhaustion she wasn't sure.

What she *did* know, however, was that tonight she intended to put to rest this insane theory that Cole was behind the thefts at the inn. The best part was her PI work should go completely unnoticed, as it was masked by an innocent delivery of his favorite meal: barbeque beef brisket.

She grabbed her things and a mammoth doggie bag—Old Tom deserved some leftovers, too—and headed into town, all the while telling herself it was the right thing to do. So why did the idea of snooping around his apartment have her feeling so guilty?

Because it's wrong, whispered her conscience.

"No more wrong than this whole town thinking he's some scary ex-con," she muttered as she pulled into her parking space behind the row of buildings that housed both their apartments. A few deep breaths, and the reminder that this would help Cole in the long run, then Maddie was out of the car and climbing Granville's back staircase.

She knocked on the door and resisted the urge to run.

Get in, look around, get out. No talking about dates or Tyson. Definitely no more kissing. Well, not unless he—

The door opened with a low whine, and Tom Granville squinted out at the dimly lit landing. "Madelyn? What brings you here at this hour?"

She glanced down at her watch and cringed. It was going on eight thirty. "Sorry to bother you, Mr. Granville, but I made brisket tonight and thought I'd bring you all some leftovers."

A broad smile stretched across his weathered face. "Ah, you know my Cole well. Come in, come in, let's get you out of the cold."

She did as she was told, scanning the interior as he closed the door behind her. Their apartment was at least twice the size of hers, which, sadly, still wasn't saying much. Old Tom's décor was that of an aging widower, mismatched furniture of varying colors and fabrics, all clean but well worn. Beyond the living room stood a round wooden table with four chairs neatly pushed in. A kitchen only slightly larger than her own but with newer appliances stood past that, its laminate seventies-gold countertops peeling at the corners.

"Please, make yourself at home while I go and get Cole. I'd holler for him, but the boy likes to practice with headphones on to keep from bothering me." Tom shook his head. "I appreciate the thought, but I swear a train could tear through this living room and he wouldn't hear it."

Maddie laughed politely and set the leftovers on his table, watching as he headed down the hall to what she assumed was Cole's room. The minute he disappeared from sight, she started looking behind furniture and inside the wide cabinets set into the wall at each side of the room's fireplace, looking for any sign of her missing utensils, Brent's missing tools, and Ruby's missing photo album.

Nothing.

Relieved, she hurried to the kitchen and started digging through cupboards and drawers. Still no sign of anything. Maddie turned back toward the living room, wanting to check the space once more for any hiding place she might have overlooked, and found Old Tom staring at her with one brow arched.

"I, uh, was just looking for a, um, fork. And knife. And maybe a plate."

Old Tom studied her a moment longer, then stepped past to produce the items she'd just lamely listed. As he did, Maddie fought the urge to fan herself. It felt like the temperature had gone up about fifteen degrees since she'd arrived. "So, where's Cole?"

"Sound asleep," Tom said, shaking his head. "Poor boy's been working himself to the bone, getting that shop ready for its grand opening."

Maddie took the offered dish and utensils from him and prepared a plate of leftovers for her host. "Did he finally set a date?"

"No. He's had a few setbacks this week. Nothing major, thankfully. I'm sure you know all about them."

"Yeah," she lied, bothered that Cole hadn't shared the stories with her. Then again, when would he have, when they'd spent so much time on her petty dating drama. Shame warmed her cheeks.

"Oh, don't worry too much about him—Cole's had lots of practice at being resilient."

"Really?" she asked, settling into a chair opposite the one Tom now took. "He never talks much about his past. Like, at all."

Mr. Granville smiled. "That's his way. Of course, if I'd grown up with Daisy Mae raising me, I'd want to leave my past in the past, too."

"Daisy Mae?"

"His mother. My daughter-in-law."

"Oh, right."

Shoot, Cole had mentioned her name before, Maddie had just forgotten. Shame pummeled her anew. Though, he hadn't spoken of her since that first time, now that she thought about it. Daisy Mae. It sounded like a pretty enough name. But there was something in the way he'd said it that left Maddie wondering.

"Was she strict or something?"

"No, quite the opposite. Daisy Mae was a dreamer, a drifter. She never liked to stay in any place for long, always after adventure. Fun."

He rose and crossed the room to retrieve a picture from one of the drawers Maddie had just checked. Shame made way for guilt—seriously, she was starting to feel like the world's worst friend—as Tom brought it to her and resumed his seat. A man and woman stared up at her from inside its frame, him tall and lean, her thin and absolutely radiant. Both wore ear-to-ear grins, the man standing behind her with his hands on her belly.

On baby bump Cole, she guessed.

"She's gorgeous," Maddie breathed, envy rearing its ugly head in her mind.

"Yes. I knew Lucas was a goner the minute he brought her home, had never seen my son look so starry-eyed before. Three weeks later they hit the road to Las Vegas to elope. After that it was Oklahoma, then Texas. Luke drove semis for a living, which suited Daisy Mae just fine. She loved being on the road, seeing the sights. When Cole came along, he rode right along with them. Until…"

Old Tom shook his head, and Maddie wished she could fast forward past this next part. Something bad had happened, she could tell from the look on his face.

"There was an accident, wasn't there?" she whispered.

"Yes. Sleet slicked roads and semis don't mix too well. Growing up in Michigan, Luke knew that full well. He tried to warn his boss, to convince them to allow him a few hours to let the ice melt away, but they wouldn't hear of it. Things were different in those days. Less regulation on over-the-road hauling."

Maddie's heart broke for Mr. Granville. In all the years she'd been at the Checkerberry, she'd never heard this story. "I'm so sorry for your loss."

"Thank you, sweetie. It was a long time ago, but the heart never fully mends when you lose a child. It's the parent who should lead the way to heaven, not the other way around."

It stinks being on the other end of it, too, she thought, the loss of her beloved grandmother coming to mind, but kept the opinion to herself.

"So, Cole and his mother—were they in the accident, too?"

"No. Thankfully, Luke had insisted they stay behind. She was devastated when the news arrived. There she was, a young mother, little schooling and no job. Eileen and I tried to convince her to move back to Mount Pleasant, to let us shoulder some of her responsibilities while she got her feet under her, but she wouldn't have it."

"So what did she do?"

He offered Maddie a sad smile. "Oh, she tried to provide for her and Cole. Got a decent job in a convenience store outside of Amarillo, found a neighbor to watch Cole while she was gone. But being in the same place day after day didn't suit Daisy Mae, and it wasn't long before she quit one job and then left another. They lived like gypsies, her and Cole, drifting from town to town. Only stayed in one place long enough to earn a little money for food; staying longer if she needed booze. Or drugs. Sometimes they'd live out of cheap motels, other times with men she called her boyfriends."

Mr. Granville shook his head. "The summer Cole turned twelve Daisy Mae was incarcerated for sixty days after being found wandering the streets, high on something or another. He came to stay with us, took most of the summer to get him to come out of his shell. Broke our hearts when his mama made parole and we had to send him back. But the law's the law."

"It seems so wrong, putting him back in that kind of an environment."

"We thought so, too. But we also knew that Cole would do his best to take care of her. And he did, right up until his eighteenth birthday. That's when the straw finally broke the camel's back."

Maddie chanced a quick glance toward the hallway. "What happened on his birthday?"

"That's the night Daisy Mae tried to rob the town liquor store. She took off from the motel they were staying at in their lone car. Cole woke a short time later after the front door she'd left cracked slammed into the entryway's wall on a gust of wind. Worried that one of her recent boyfriends had taken off with her, Cole got dressed, grabbed his daddy's old handgun that I'd given him, and ran into town. He couldn't understand why the car was parked on the sidewalk beside the town's liquor store, but heard a crash and raced inside, fearing the worst.

"What he found, however, was his mama, high on lord knows what, trying to drag heavy crates of whiskey out the back door. As he was trying to talk Daisy Mae out of doing what she was doing, the police arrived."

Maddie grimaced. "Let me guess. They found him carrying

a concealed weapon and assumed the worst."

Old Tom nodded.

"But he was innocent!"

"Unfortunately, it was his word against theirs."

Maddie ran a hand over her hair. "But Daisy Mae—didn't she tell them he wasn't a part of it?"

Mr. Granville folded his hands before him on the table's edge. "Cole's never told me exactly what was said that night. Judging by the fact that he was hauled off to jail for assisting in an armed robbery, however, I have to assume she did him no favors."

"Armed robbery!" Maddie struggled to control her anger. "After all he'd done for her, he ends up going to jail? Please at least tell me she did time, too?"

"Oh yes. While Cole's prior record was clean, her past laundry list of charges increased her sentence. Even on good behavior, she'll be in jail for another five years or so."

Jail. Poor Cole had been sent to jail, ironically for a crime he was trying to prevent his good-for-nothing mother from committing. The unfairness of it all nearly brought her to tears.

"How long was he in for?" she asked softly.

"Three years, then probation for another three. The day he walked out of the courtroom a free man, I was there waiting to bring him back home to Mount Pleasant. In Texas, he'd forever have that dark cloud hanging over his head. But up here…here he has a chance to start over."

Except the rumors of his past, ill-conceived and twisted for maximum dramatic effect, were threatening all of that. Her heart broke for him a little bit more.

"Thank you for telling me," she said.

Old Tom nodded. "My grandson's no hardened criminal, Madelyn. Nor a thief. He's a good man with a heart the size of Texas that's been trodden on for far too long."

Maddie nodded and shifted her gaze to the hallway.

"Do you mind if I go back and see him before I go?"

"Last door on the left. While you do that, I'm going to reheat this plate full of brisket you served me. It smells delicious."

She offered him a wink, then made her way toward Cole's room. Maddie paused at the door, debating whether or not to knock, but discovered it already ajar. A quick peek inside found Cole sprawled on his back atop an old patchwork quilt covering his still-made bed, eyes closed and breathing slow and steady.

Quiet as a mouse, she slid past the door and looked around the room for an extra blanket to cover him with, no longer bothering to scope the place out for stolen goods. She'd suspected before arriving here tonight that she wouldn't find anything. Now she was certain.

No blanket in sight, she lifted one corner of the quilt beneath him and carefully folded it up and over him.

Like a giant Cole burrito, she thought and snorted a giggle.

Cole's lashes fluttered open. He blinked a few times, brows furrowing as he lifted his head off the pillow. "Maddie? What is it? Am I late for work?"

"Shh, you're all right. I brought you some leftover barbeque brisket."

With a smile, he sank back into his pillow. "No kidding? That's my favorite."

"I know. It'll be here when you wake up in the morning."

She reached up to brush a hair from his face and tucked it behind his ear. It killed her to think of him as the little boy in Old Tom's story, dragged from town to town without getting to experience a normal childhood. And yet, rather than grow cold and bitter at the unfairness of it all, Cole had remained a caring soul. Heck, he was one of the kindest people she knew. Kindest to her, anyway. Some days, that was a monumental feat all on its own.

His eyes drifted shut once more. She perched on the edge of his bed and stroked his cheek, wishing she could erase his past, extinguish the rumors, yet was powerless to do so. With a sigh, she drew her hand back and made to leave. But Cole's hand came up to claim hers.

"Stay. Just a little longer."

"Okay," she whispered, giving his hand a small squeeze. "But only until you fall asleep."

A sleepy smile tugged at his perfect lips. "You're the best, Maddie."

"I know."

He cracked one eye open. "And modest, too."

"Of course."

She chuckled softly and watched his lid slide shut and breathing even out once more. And in that moment, she knew it was hopeless to try and deny the feelings she had for him any longer. If anything, the discovery of his past had strengthened her feelings toward him, not scared her away. Which meant it was probably good she'd weenied out again last night and not asked Tyson to the gala.

With a sigh, she realized she'd fallen for the coach, and now had a semi-lured in boyfriend to set free. This was why it was easier not to date. To stay at home and watch Fido bonk his face into the side of his bowl repeatedly while the world went right on by.

But now, savoring the warmth of Cole's hand as it covered her own, she knew she was all talk, spoken or otherwise. Because the way she felt in this moment, needed, appreciated? Well, she'd take that over sitting home alone any day.

Now if only she could find a way to make it last…

Chapter Sixteen

Cole hit the sidewalk Monday morning with brisket in his belly and Maddie consuming his thoughts. But unlike usual, he didn't try to push her image away. She'd come to check on him last night, had brought him peace after a tiring and emotionally turbulent day. He couldn't remember the last time he'd slept so well, knowing she would stay if only for a little longer.

Because she cared.

His heart swelled in his chest and he drew in a deep breath of brisk October downtown air. Yeah, it tasted awful. Yeah, the cold bit his lungs. But who could complain when life was finally starting to look up?

Though, there was the whole matter of Tyson. From what he could get out of Maddie, things between them still hadn't clicked. Would it be wrong to step in and swipe her out from under his nose? As he pondered the thought, conflicted, a couple emerged from a shop ahead of him. He had his arm around her, she was snuggled into his side to keep warm. Their laughter echoed on the brick storefronts around them.

That. That's what Cole wanted. Someone to laugh with, to hold close, to adore. To be adored by. He'd denied himself the chance for too long, afraid his past would drive them away. But the bandage had been ripped off thanks to Sheridan Realty, his past fueling the town's rumor mill. Maddie had to have heard something by now. And yet she hadn't shunned him, hadn't treated him any differently than usual.

Maybe it was time to tell her the truth. Surely she would understand. And if she didn't, well, then it was never meant to be.

Tonight. I'll tell her tonight.

Determination lifted an invisible weight long carried on his shoulders, and Cole resisted the urge to run off and buy her flowers. No, it was too soon for that. Better to be honest with her, gauge her reaction, then see if she felt the same way about him as he felt of her. Because there was no denying it—he was falling for Maddie, harder every day.

If only his new shop would hurry up and get off the ground. He knew it would take time. Heck, his grandfather warned him it could take months, even a year before business settled into a predictable routine. But these rumors weren't helping matters any.

A man stepped out of the shop beside his as he approached and offered him a tight smile. "Morning, Granville."

"Morning, Mr. Smith." Cole racked his brain, trying to think of the aging frame maker's first name. Sam? Walter? Whatever it was, Mr. Smith had been none-too-pleased to learn that a guitar store was going in on their quiet street. Had expressed his concerns about the noise nearly every day since Cole first put signs up in the window, advertising lesson opportunities. To date, he'd kept the noise low and always on the opposite side of the shop, so he had no idea what had Mr. Smith scowling like an English Bulldog this morning.

"Seems someone tripped the alarm last night. Yours, then

mine."

"Oh no." Cole's gaze shifted to his shop. The window was intact, the front display looking unblemished. "Was anything taken from your place?"

"No, but I thought you should know so you can look yours over."

"Thanks a lot." Cole headed for his door but paused when he realized Smith was following.

"I don't really care what you do in that shop of yours," Smith said in a low voice. "Or what you've gotten yourself into in the past. But this shop is all I have. If you're mixed up in some kind of trouble, well, you'd best be taking it elsewhere."

With that, the man turned and shuffled back into the Frame Gallery, the door snicking shut behind him. After a moment, Cole shook off his surprise and turned toward his own place. It was going to take more than tripped alarms and scowling shop owners to keep him from his dreams. Robberies, however, would be tougher to overcome.

"Nice talk, Smith," he muttered under his breath. "Let's not do it again any time soon."

...

Maddie climbed the steps to her apartment Monday night, looking forward to a long, hot soak in the tub. Her place might be the size of a postage stamp, and far from glamorous, but in the tub she could close her eyes and pretend she was anywhere. Tonight, her imagined destination would probably also harbor one too-sexy-for-his-own-good southern boy, who'd consumed her thoughts most of the day as it was.

But when she drew near the landing and spied a pair of familiar cowboy boots perched on the second to top step, daydreaming took a back seat to worry. And maybe a bit of embarrassment, over being caught thinking about him.

"Cole? What are you doing here?"

A half grin, but still he did not rise. "Guess I lost my way."

Worry rattled her again. Something was bothering him, something pretty big for him to be sitting here, waiting for her. She decided to play dumb, let him talk when he was good and ready.

"Well, can you lose it a little to the left? I'd like to get inside and out of these shoes."

His right brow twitched as he shifted on the step, his gaze following her as she brushed by. Maddie felt her cheeks warm. *Ha, as if I had a chance.* The very thought of her, Cole, and clothes coming off, though, had her all sorts of flustered. She fumbled with her key not once but twice, then struggled to put enough weight behind her usual door-shouldering maneuver.

"Here, let me get that for you."

Cole rose and came to stand beside her, his tall, lean frame easing into what little space was left. She squeezed against the outer wall, trying to give him room, and savored the scent of his cologne. Lord, he smelled good. All sandalwood and man.

You should be thinking of Tyson, whispered her conscience.

You should shut the hell up, she mentally whispered back.

With a grunt and twist, the door was opened all too soon. Maddie offered him a smile and led the way inside, flipping the light switch as she wondered what they'd talk about tonight. One of his new students? A story from his past? Maybe a confession about what really happened the night of his eighteenth birthday?

The door clicked shut behind her. Maddie tossed her purse into its usual spot on the counter and turned to ask how his day was. The light flicked off and suddenly Cole was there, standing less than an arm's length away, hiding in the shadows cast by the room's tiny nightlight. Oh yeah, something was definitely wrong.

"You want to talk about it?" she whispered, reaching out to brush a thumb across his cheek. Even in the dark she could see the dark circles under his eyes.

Cole leaned into her touch and raised a hand to cover hers. "Not really."

"Long day?"

He snorted. "More like long life."

"So I've heard."

His eyes narrowed. "You did, did you?"

She nodded, brushing her thumb across his cheek again. "Whatever they told you…it wasn't true."

"You calling your grandfather a liar?" She grinned.

"My grandfather? When did you…?" Understanding dawned on his face. "Last night. The brisket."

Maddie shrugged. "We had a few minutes to kill. He cares a great deal for you, you know."

"And you?"

"I guess Tom and I have gotten along well enough in the past."

Cole chuckled and moved his hand from over hers to the small of her back. "I mean do you care a great deal about me, too?"

Crap. Apparently it was confessional night at the Frye house. As much as she wanted to change the subject, or throw out a snarky comment to distract him, she couldn't. She wouldn't. Instead, she met his gaze and nodded.

"Even knowing what you do about me? About my past?"

"You were innocent, Cole. Trying to do the right thing. It just…"

"Backfired."

"Horribly," she added with a grimace.

But rather than be bothered by her added commentary, a look of relief settled over his features. Cole drew her close and placed a cheek to the crown of her head. Maddie wrapped her arms around him, savoring his warmth.

"It's been so long since anyone has looked at me without judgment in their eyes," he whispered. "I don't want to lose your friendship, Maddie."

Friendship. Though it shouldn't have, his comment stung, confirming her earlier suspicion. Coworkers? Yes. Friends? Absolutely. Lovers? Not in the cards. But she'd just have to learn to be okay with that, because she'd grown far too fond of him to want to lose what they did have together.

"You won't."

He drew back, his gaze searching hers. For what, exactly, she didn't know. She was here, wasn't she?

Cole's gaze shifted to her lips.

Friends, she reminded herself. *Don't let your imagination run wild.*

His hand snaked into her hair, freed after her shift of its usual messy bun, to gently cup the nape of her neck. Okay, so this wasn't something she'd done with other male friends. Maybe it was a Texas thing?

"I've fallen for you, Maddie." His lips lowered to within a whisper of hers. "Coaching be damned, I want you all to myself."

Maddie stood there in utter shock. Had she heard him right, or was this all some grand illusion?

"Really?"

"Mmm-hmm." He pressed a soft kiss to her lips, to her cheek, to the hollow beneath her ear.

"But I'm—"

"Don't." He drew back, his face unusually serious. "Whatever it is you were going to say, it's a lie, all a lie you keep telling yourself. You're not too fat, too thin, too short, too tall. You're not too intimidating, too confident, too curvy. You are 100 percent real in a world full of imposters and fakes, and I think that makes you absolutely perfect."

"But...you haven't seen all of me."

A crooked smile stretched his perfect lips. "We can remedy that, you know."

"What, now? *Tonight*?"

She stepped away to collect her thoughts and looked to her bedroom door. Had she made the bed this morning? Picked up the dirty clothes off the floor?

Shaved her legs?

"Unless, of course, you don't want to." His words said he understood, but his tone was thick with desire.

The same desire she'd been fighting since he'd stepped foot into her kitchen.

"I do. Of course I do, it's just..." She wrung her hands, grateful for the dark. Darn, a little notice before springing this on her would have been nice. Time to mentally prepare.

"You're nervous."

"Well, duh." A nervous laugh escaped her.

"Then how about we take it slow for now? Go with the flow?"

He took her hand and pulled Maddie into his arms. His velvet voice greeted her ears as Cole began quietly singing a Journey song she'd admitted to being one of her favorites the last night they'd worked together, and the two began swaying to their own private dance. She rested her head on his shoulder and closed her eyes.

Oh yeah, she'd take this over some stuffy gala any day.

His hands slid to her hips, and a shiver rattled through her. They felt...good there. Right. Her mind began to race, thinking of other places those skilled hands would feel. Even as those thoughts filled her mind, the doubts and insecurities of her past tried to claw their way to the forefront.

No. That was then, this was now. Cole had fallen for her. *Her*! And he'd just called her absolutely perfect. If that wasn't a confidence builder, what was? If a guy like Cole said he wanted her, then it was high time she learned to listen and let go of her past.

"I've always loved your voice," Maddie said as the song came to a close.

"You do?"

"Mmm-hmm. Could listen to it all night long."

Cole bent to press a kiss to the hollow beneath her ear. "All night long, huh?"

"Yes," she whispered. "Maybe that, um, remedy of yours is something I'd like to learn more about."

"Oh yeah?"

He pulled back to study her for long moment, his big, blue eyes heavy-lidded with desire. She dug deep for her bravado and slipped out of his grasp, angling for the kitchen. "Uh huh."

"Um, Maddie? If memory serves, the bedroom is that way."

"You're right." She plucked her cell phone from her purse and sent a quick message to Kayla, asking her to cover breakfast in the morning. Everything was prepped and ready to go, nothing but pastries and cereal planned, anyway. Message sent, she returned to Cole. "And now we won't have to rush what happens in there nearly as much."

"I rather like the sound of that."

He pulled her close and sealed his approval with a kiss. And another. And another. He really was the best kisser she'd ever met. She would have gladly stood there all night, making out in her dining room, if she hadn't already spent the past few hours on her feet.

"Cole?"

"Hmm?" he asked, his lips softly gliding over her own.

"I really would like to get out of these shoes now."

He chuckled, the sound warming her far more than any heater could in this lonely old apartment.

"Right. How about you lead the way, and I'll help you

with that."

Maddie liked the sound of that. Yes, she was scared out of her mind—it'd been forever and a day since anyone had seen her naked, let alone touched her. But this was Cole, the sweetest, most caring man she knew. She had no doubt in anything they did together he'd treat her like royalty, bedroom adventures included.

That thought kept her from making a run for it. Instead, she intertwined her fingers with his and led the way toward her bedroom.

"I'd love it if you would."

Chapter Seventeen

A creak and dip in the bed woke Cole before sunrise the next morning, followed by the brush of soft lips to his forehead. Maddie's sweet perfume filled his senses, and he worked to pry his eyes open. She sat beside him on the bed, dressed in her usual chef outfit and looking far more awake than him.

"I thought you said someone was covering the morning shift?" he asked.

"Me, too," she said. "Unfortunately, my backup has been throwing up half the night. Can't have germs like that in my kitchen."

"I say let 'em eat cold cereal or something. I'd make it worth your while." He raised one brow, though struggling to stay awake.

"Even then, someone's got to set it all out." She laughed softly. "Besides, you'll be asleep before I walk out the door."

"Not if you ditch those clothes and climb back in bed with me."

"You know I can't," she whispered, cupping his cheek. "Besides, if I didn't come into work, Ruby would probably send someone over to check on me. And then we'd probably both get fired. I'd hate for that to happen."

He sighed and lay back against the pillow, letting his eyelids drift shut. "You might be onto something there."

"Stay as long as you like, I've got a fresh pot of coffee set to brew in another hour or two."

"Thanks."

"No, thank you. For…everything."

And thank you for making last night the best of my life.

That's what he wanted to say, anyway, but the words got stuck in his throat. Instead all he could manage was a whispered, "Anytime, Maddie."

Her lips brushed against his, light as a feather, then warmed a trail up to his ear. "You know I'm going to hold you to that, right?"

"I'd be disappointed if you didn't."

"Me, too." She drew back. "Hey, Cole?"

He cracked one eye back open at the hesitation in her voice. "Yeah?"

"You…don't need to call your grandpa or anything, do you?"

"No I left him a note, saying where I'd be."

"Oh, great. Reverend Granville's gonna love that."

Cole grinned and slid his hand around her waist, trying to resist the temptation to pull her back on top of him. "Nah, I said you were scared of the dark and asked me to come over for protection."

"You mean come over *with* protection."

At that, he laughed. "Good thing I stocked up, huh?"

"Absolutely."

Pink tinted her cheeks. She looked amazing this morning, her usual stoic facade absent, replaced with a soft, happy glow. Would the others notice at work today, her waltzing in and acting like she was still on cloud nine? Would she confess to their night of loving making, that he'd done all he could to kiss away any doubts she'd had of her wonderful curves and the affect they'd had on him from day one?

Did he really care?

Nope, not a bit.

"I'll be sure to restock before tonight."

"What's tonight?"

"When I come back over for an encore performance." She chuckled and he curled his body around hers. "What, you don't really think my grandfather will believe I cured you of your fear of the dark in just one night, do you?"

"I think I'd better go and hope your grandfather doesn't think too much about any of it."

She pressed one last kiss to his forehead, muttering something about "surely going to hell," then pecked him a quick kiss on the cheek. Cole puckered up, and she planted one last kiss on his lips as well. Then she was gone, off to save the world one pancake at a time. He rolled back over and let sleep pull him under once more, succumbing to dreams about beautiful towns with autumn leaves, Maddie snuggled beside him on a park bench in the sunshine, them sitting together watching happy, smiling passersby.

Unfortunately, the dream quickly faded, replaced by one far gloomier and eerily like the reality he'd been living the past few days. He awoke disoriented and unsettled, trying to brush it off. Because he'd lived too much of that for too long. Until last night, that is. Last night had easily been the best of his life. And not just because of what he and Maddie had done, but because there, in her arms, nothing else seemed to matter. Not his future, not the past, only the there and now.

It'd been incredibly freeing.

Memories of their night together filled his mind, and Cole gave up on going back to sleep this time. He rolled out of bed with a smile, downed a quick cup of coffee while watching

Fido ram his fish lips into the side of his bowl—seriously, man, what was up that?—and then headed home to shower and change.

By the time he headed toward his shop, a bright orange sun was lifting off from the horizon. It was like an omen, a sign that today was a day full of possibilities. He strode around the last corner between home and his shop, looking forward to seeing Maddie at work later but trying to think through how to act around her without being too obvious about the step they'd taken together last night, and drew to an abrupt stop. Up ahead sat his storefront, its glass frontage covered in large, blood red letters. A message, no doubt, intended for him:

Go back to Texas, Jailbird.

...

Maddie glared at the noonday news Tuesday, ready to take on the town. Or at least that nosey Amber Jensen, Channel 10's obnoxious field correspondent. Someone had called in about Cole's shop being defaced, and instead of criticizing the vandals, prissy Amber had strutted up to Cole—on a ladder, sponge in one hand and bucket of soapy water in the other—and demanded to know why he was bringing such chaos to "our quiet town."

"You want chaos, woman?" Maddie muttered. "I'll show you chaos."

Ruby looked up from her napkin-folding at the end of the bar in surprise. "What's that, dear?"

The dining room was empty of all but staff today, the inn's fall occupancy rates beginning to taper off and their current guests early eaters. Otherwise, she never would have turned on the flat screen television Brent had installed this summer behind the bar. Good for the sports fans, he'd said. *Or for putting arrogant twit news reporters on display.* Maddie shot the television another dirty look as Miles emerged from the hallway leading back to his office.

"Can I have the afternoon off, Ruby? I need to have words with that stuck-up news reporter on Channel 10."

Miles took a seat next to his grandmother. "What's your beef with Amber?"

"My beef," said Maddie, "is that she's harassing Cole, who is clearly the victim here."

"Victim? What are you talking about?"

"Someone vandalized Cole's shop again this morning," said Ruby. "Wrote a despicable message in big bold letters for the whole town to see."

"Oh, wow. Poor kid can't catch a break." Miles shook his head.

Maddie pointed to the dark television. "Not with the town treating him like yesterday's garbage. Seriously, how can these people live with themselves?"

"People shun what they don't understand, dear. It's no different here than many other towns across the country."

"But it's not right, Ruby. Here he is, trying to make a decent living, to teach people music, for crying out loud, and we're shunning him like he's some crazy former psychopath."

Miles reached for a ham sandwich from the tray Maddie'd left on the counter with a shrug. "Maybe he is."

"Maybe you should take that back."

"Madelyn Frye." It wasn't unusual for Ruby to call her by her given name. But when she threw in a last name as well, anyone close to the Mastersons knew a lecture was sure to follow. "I'll not have threats of violence here in my inn. Miles, you will apologize to Maddie for your snide remark."

"But—"

"Apologize."

He cast Maddie a dark look. "Sorry. For insinuating the obvious," he added with a mumble.

"Now, Maddie, you apologize to Miles."

She threw him an even darker look. "Sorry that I know the real story and you don't."

Miles's right brow arched. "Is that so?"

"Yes." She crossed her arms. "According to his grandfather, Cole is neither an axe murderer nor a thief. Well, not a thief for sure. Honestly, I didn't ask about any murders."

"So if he didn't steal and he didn't kill anyone, why the heck is everyone saying he spent time in prison?"

"Because he did," she said, her gaze drifting back to the television screen. Had he been all over the news that day, too? Blasphemed for a misunderstood role in his mother's crime? "His only fault, though, was being in the wrong place at the wrong time. Cole was trying to stop his strung out mom from robbing a liquor store."

"Man, I'm sorry, Maddie." Miles ran a hand through his hair. "I've been riding you about the guy for a while now. Guess I let the rumors and suspicion get to me, too."

"Yeah, well, now you know better."

"Thomas always believed in the boy, said he had a good heart. His mama, though, I remember her. She was something else altogether." Ruby shook her head, frowning.

"Guys, we've got to do something to help him. These rumors are getting out of hand. Much more, and those jerks might run him right out of town."

"Probably their intent," said Miles.

"Then help me." Maddie threw him a pleading look. "Help *him*."

Miles took a bite of his sandwich and leaned back, assuming the classic Miles "analyzing the situation" pose. Ruby stopped with her napkin folding, brows drawn low in concentration as well. Maddie looked between the two of them, waiting for an idea to surface.

"What happened?" Brent strode in with Kayla close

behind. "The last time you all looked this serious, Uncle Albert had died."

"Small-mindedness is what happened." Maddie flicked the TV back on. "Someone vandalized Cole's shop, left him a nasty message in big red letters. Only they've got the story wrong. He was innocent, just didn't have anyone in his corner to convince the jury. Now Little Miss Jensen on Channel 10 is having a heyday vilifying Cole who is 'putting the town in unease.'"

Kayla shot Miles a dirty look.

"What?" he said. "It's not like I told her to do that. Heck, we only went out on one date."

"Thank heavens for that," Ruby mumbled.

"So, do the police have any idea who's behind this?"

Maddie ran a hand over her hair. "No. And honestly? I don't think they care. So far, they've chalked all the eggings up to rowdy teenagers. I half wonder if they aren't all secretly hoping he packs his bags and leaves."

"Well, we can't have that." Kayla placed a hand on Maddie's shoulder.

"Wait a minute." Ruby leaned forward, her gaze roving between them. "There's more going on here than you're both telling us. Ladies?"

Maddie felt Kayla give her shoulder a gentle squeeze. What to do? Lie and say there was no more, and risk the Mastersons not doing all they could to help Cole, or admit her feelings—and put his job in jeopardy—and hope they would all pull together to save him from the town mob? She let out a long sigh.

"I..."

"You fell for him."

All eyes widened in surprise and shifted to Brent, who turned up his hands. "What? It was bound to happen. Seriously, was I the only one who saw this coming?"

Miles faked a cough to cover up his laugh, and Maddie threw him a warning look. *Stupid camera...*

"Fine, yes, it happened all right? Hard not to, with all you ridiculous lovebirds flitting about the place."

"Oh, whatever," said Miles. "Wait—what about this other guy, the one you're bringing to the gala?"

She looked to the floor and shrugged. "It didn't work out."

"Kissing coworkers *and* breaking hearts." He shook his head. "It's like I don't even know you anymore."

Maddie swiped a folded napkin and chucked it at Miles, who easily dodged it, laughing. His grandmother shot him a warning look, and the mood at the table sobered once more. Maddie dropped onto a bar stool and looked to the others.

"Needless to say, I'm worried about Cole. And maybe feeling a bit...protective of him. But no matter what happens between us, he deserves a fresh start here in Mount Pleasant."

"Who else knows about his past?" asked Brent.

"I'm not sure. Heck, I didn't even know it until Old Tom filled me in the other day. I mean, sure, it's probably all public record, but you'd have to be looking to find that kind of dirt on someone."

"Like someone with a vengeance." Kayla fell quiet for a moment, then looked to the family matriarch. "Ruby, do you think I could borrow Brent for the rest of the afternoon? I think I have an idea."

"Of course, dear. What is it you two plan to do?"

Kayla looked from Brent to Maddie, determination in her eyes. "Some digital sightseeing."

...

Cole heard his cell buzz from its place on his makeshift dresser and sighed. No doubt it was Maddie, checking up on him yet again. He didn't have the heart to tell her it was a pay-as-you-go plan and she was eating up all his minutes. Heck, at this point, he didn't have the heart to do much more than play the blues.

Because that's what he was living—the blues.

How you holding up? her text read.

Yep, checking on him again. Yesterday, the knowledge that she cared, that she was worried about him, would have warmed him from the inside out. But ever since finding that hate message plastered all over his shop this morning, he'd struggled to shake off the chill of rejection.

He never should have signed that lease.

I have dinner waiting over here for you. And dessert.

His stomach growled in response, unhappy that he'd hid in his room most of the evening. With the inn's business slowing down, though, Miles had asked to trim Cole's hours to only Wednesday through Saturday. With only a few weeks left until they closed for the season, and with a nearly empty inn, even that might be a stretch.

Which didn't bode well for Cole's wallet.

Instead of mope in the living room or down in the shop, he'd holed up in his room. While he loved his grandfather, today wasn't a good one for hearing the usual lecture about facing his past and moving on. Because it was growing abundantly clear that there *was* no moving on, not in a town like this. Trouble was, he didn't know a town that wasn't like this. Cole would be stuck working crap jobs the rest of his life, all thanks to his dear old mom.

And Maddie deserved so much better.

Frustrated at the quicksand he called life, Cole set his guitar on its stand, grabbed his jacket, and headed for the door.

"I'm going out for a bit, Grandpa," he called.

Silence answered.

Must be in bed already, Cole thought. Though, a quick

glance at the microwave clock found it to be only eight. Worry clawed at him—it wasn't like Old Tom not to answer. Cole checked his room, the bathroom, then looked out the small window at the end of the hall. Relief washed over him to see the delivery truck was gone. It'd kill him to find his grandfather...

No, he wouldn't let himself think like that. Old Tom was sharp as a porcupine's quill and spry as a jack rabbit; his end was nowhere near in sight. Besides, he had a medical alert bracelet, caring neighbors, and a town full of friends—if his grandfather so much as hiccupped wrong, someone would know and rush to the rescue.

What would that be like, Cole wondered as he made his way down their set of stairs, out to the sidewalk, and then up the flight leading to Maddie. To have friends and acquaintances who looked out for you instead of looked out because of you?

Maddie opened the door nearly the second he knocked, and once she'd shouldered the damn thing open stepped out to pull him into a tight hug.

"I've worried about you all day."

And there was his answer. At her touch, her voice, he nearly cried. How could he stick around, knowing the blight he was bound to bring to her reputation?

Selfishly, he stayed, if only for tonight.

"No need to worry," he lied, voice thick with more emotion than he would have liked. "I'm a big boy."

"A big boy who's had a hornet's nest dropped on his head." She drew back, fury clear on her face. "I about stormed downtown at lunch and clawed that reporter's eyes out."

Cole chuckled and led her forward, then muscled the door shut behind them. "Remind me never to piss you off."

"I'm serious, Cole. Like you didn't have enough going on with the graffiti? She's all, 'Look at me, I'm so cute and lalala,' while this town's dragging you through hell and back."

Yep, pretty much. "Not the first time, Madds. Fairly certain it won't be the last."

"Well, we're working to remedy that. In the meantime, come eat."

Not understanding but starved, he did as she ordered, savoring every bite of the meal and every story that she told. Cole remained quiet, shoveling food in—okay, he was more hungry than he'd realized—and nodding where appropriate. Full from the lasagna and melt-in-your-mouth garlic bread, he passed on the key lime pie. Maddie's shoulders sank.

"Maybe later," he promised.

She nodded, not meeting his eyes.

Great, now he'd gone and upset her. *Nothing like being the town outcast, bringing misery everywhere you go...*

"You wanna play cards or something?" she asked, her back to him as she stowed their untouched dessert away. "Watch some TV?"

Cole slipped off his seat and took a new one on her tattered couch, then patted the space beside him. "Nope. I wanna sit here with my girl, listening to her musical voice as she tells me about her favorite childhood adventures."

She cast him a confused, wary look. "You feeling all right?"

"Yeah, why?"

"Because *you're* the one with the musical voice." She shook her head and took a seat at the opposite end of the couch, drawing a pillow onto her lap. "And my childhood had no adventures, which is why I turned out to be the sharp-tongued smarmy-pants I am today. Now lay down."

"I'm fine, really."

"Lay. Down. You look exhausted."

He was, mentally and physically, and so argued no more. When he cast her a questioning look, she ordered him to close his eyes and relax. Again, he did as he was told. Her fingers pressed gently above the bridge of his nose, slid up and over his brows, and came to rest at his temples. As she moved, the scents from tonight's kitchen work stirred in the air around them.

Garlic. Parmesan. Cloves. Something citrusy.

Up, over, hold. Up, over, hold. The stress he'd been carrying in his shoulders began to slip away.

"Tell me a story," he whispered, fearful he'd fall asleep if the silence continued.

"A story? Hmm. Once upon a time, there lived a fairy princess in a castle far, far away."

He lifted a brow and chanced a look at Maddie. She frowned and pushed his brow back into place. "My choice, so deal with it."

A smile tugged at his lips. She had that effect on him.

"Close your eyes. I can't focus with you looking at me like that."

"Like what?"

Her mouth quirked at one corner. "Like *that*. Now quit."

"Fine." He closed both eyes, then cracked one back open, just to goad her.

"*Cole…*"

He chuckled, allowing the open lid to drift shut. "Yes, ma'am. But I have to know—does this story have a happy ending?"

"Of course," she whispered, stroking his face even more gently than before. "Fairy tales always do."

Chapter Eighteen

Maddie woke to the sound of her alarm clock going off in the next room and a horrific kink in her neck. In her lap remained Cole, curled on his side so that he was facing her, his features relaxed and peaceful. They wouldn't be, though, if that darned alarm blared much longer.

She eased out from under him, careful not to let his head roll free from the pillow, and hurried off to silence the alarm. The kink in her neck intensified as she tried to straighten, and she bit back a cry. With a scowl she grabbed today's clothes and headed for the shower, praying the hot water would help.

If he'd eaten the pie, her bed is where they would have ended up, not the couch. Good thing Key lime kept for a few days, because she darned well intended to get him back into bed. After breaking her dry spell two nights ago, Maddie had no intention of returning to the land of abstinence, not while Cole was around. Her memory drifted back to their night together as she stood beneath the shower's healing stream. No man had ever looked at her the way he did, admiring every curve and line to her body. And not in a mocking or patronizing way, either. What his eyes said was backed up by his actions, so gentle, so...thorough.

She let out a long, appreciative sigh.

But life was kicking his butt right now, so she understood why things had played out the way they did last night. He might not be used to having someone on his side, fighting for him, but Maddie was bound and determined to do exactly that. To bring him the peace and acceptance he deserved.

To bring his smile back, the way he'd helped her rediscover hers. But how?

She spent the breakfast shift recapping all she knew, searching for any hint as to who might be behind Cole's persecution. There'd been a thief in their midst at the Checkerberry up until the cameras had gone in. Since then, nothing new had been taken. A fluke coincidence, maybe a klepto guest in their midst?

Not likely. No one had stayed more than a week and the disappearing items had spanned several. So what changed? Did the thief taking the money get them what they wanted? Or had they shifted their attention to a new target?

Heck yeah, they had: Cole's shop. Ever since the thefts had stopped here, the eggings and vandalism had started there. But why? Who could possibly be that opposed to a new guitar shop in town? Or to Cole, for that matter?

Her phone buzzed, and Maddie snatched it up, eager to try and get a read on his mood today. But the text waiting wasn't from him, it was from Tyson.

Hey, beautiful. Smoothies this afternoon?

Shoot. With all of Cole's drama, she'd forgotten about Tyson. Guilt rattled her, then rattled harder as memories of her night with Cole rushed in again. All these years with no boyfriend, and now she found herself juggling two guys at once.

Sorry, have to work, she wrote back. *I also need to figure out a way to let you down easy, buddy, but I'll have to do that in person…*

A sad face emoji appeared on her screen. From a guy as big as a Mack truck. Amusing, if nothing else.

I KNOW, BUT HEY IT'S NEARLY LAUNDRY DAY.

She grimaced. Would things get weird between them at the Quarter Clean-It? If that happened, she'd just have to switch days. Or maybe put her laundry into the machines and then go hide in her apartment across the street while waiting on the rinse cycle to finish…

TRUE. K, CU SOON. NEED TO TALK TO U ABOUT SOMETHING.

Need to talk about what? Maddie responded OKAY and tossed her phone aside before he did something cheesy like sent some kissy-faced graphic. She could do romance, but cutesy texts weren't really her thing. Maybe it was good she was ending things with him now. Once a guy got on her nerves, it was hard to hold back the snark for long, and she hated to do that to the guy out of guilt if nothing else.

"Hey, Maddie, got a minute?"

She turned to see Kayla poking her head through the kitchen doors. "Sure, what's up?"

"Quick meeting in Ruby's office. Shouldn't take long."

"Oh?" She wiped her hands on her apron and started forward with a frown. "Did something else go missing?"

"Nope. More like something's been found."

Ten minutes later, Maddie was squinting at the computer screen in Ruby's office, trying to identify the graffiti artist who'd struck at the inn last night. She'd driven right past the gold letters plastered on the driveway side of the building, the color too close to the inn's pale yellow to draw her attention in the dark this morning. But the others had arrived later, the words more pronounced in the daylight.

"Bastard," she grumbled, leaning forward and clicking to restart the video.

Oh sure, the perp thought they were clever, parking at Hank Billings's place next door and walking across the field that separated it from the inn. But what they hadn't counted on was Kayla's camera position, or the motion sensor lights Brent had installed on the porch.

Unfortunately, the lights hadn't triggered until after the spray painting had been done. Still, the camera had caught the retreating figure in full color, and now as Maddie watched the video play a second time, she recognized both the black hoodie with hot pink accents and the body shape who wore it.

"Sarah," she breathed.

"What?" Miles leaned around her and grabbed the computer mouse to replay it for himself. "Are you sure?"

"Positive," said Maddie. "Too bad there's no clear shot of her face, though. The police won't do much without more proof."

"What about a search warrant?" Kayla asked. "If she took your things, Maddie, and Ruby's photo album, they should be easy enough to find."

"Yeah, if they were at her apartment. But I doubt she'd be that stupid." Maddie frowned. "I know she was mad about getting fired, but why retaliate against Cole? Why not me?"

"He did take her job," said Brent. "Though, how she knew about his rap sheet is beyond me."

"Sheridan Realty." All eyes turned to Ruby, who looked to the ceiling shaking her head. "Her grandfather is Robert Sheridan, the owner. He brought her on part time after we let her go. Perhaps she was the one who pulled his background check and credit report."

"That conniving little—"

"How'd you know that, Ruby?" said Kayla, cutting Maddie off before she said something in front of her boss she might regret.

The old innkeeper smiled. "I play bridge with half the

town's elders, dear. There's not much that goes on around here I don't know."

"But it doesn't make any sense." Maddie ran a hand over her hair. "If he opened a successful shop, logic would have it that he'd eventually quit here. I'd think she would want to help him succeed, not harass him right out of business."

"Yes, but you're talking logic and Sarah in the same sentence. And from what you've said about her in the past," said Miles, "never the two shall mix."

Maddie shook her head. "I don't know, Miles. I just have this feeling there's something more. Something we've overlooked."

He shrugged. "Maybe so, but this video still doesn't help us get her off Cole's back."

"Actually," said Brent. "Maybe it does. Madds, what kind of car does Sarah drive?"

"A black Dodge Dart. Why?"

"Bingo." He and Kayla exchanged a fist bump. "Kay and I went into town yesterday, asking other shop owners in the vicinity if any of them had surveillance cameras. Her brother Tommy's shop is near there, so we already knew of a few. Unfortunately for us, only one had video footage easily accessible. They were too far from Cole's shop to see the actual vandalism, but someone in a dark hoodie stepped out of a parked car behind their shop, threw a backpack over their shoulder, then hopped a privacy fence in the direction of Granville Guitars. Same person came back a short while later, emptied something in the dumpster, then drove off in that car."

"Let me guess," Miles said. "It was a black Dodge Dart."

"Yup."

"What about the other shops?" Maddie looked to Kayla. "The ones that didn't have instant access?"

"Brent and I are going back today to see if any were able

to pull the footage from that night. Hopefully, we'll have good news by dinnertime."

Good news for them, but catching Sarah wouldn't allay the fears and prejudice already triggered all over town toward Cole. If only there was a giant do-over button, something that could wipe the slate clean and bring him some peace in a matter of days not months or years. Plus, all this bad publicity had been brutal to his sales and lesson roster. With the inn set to close in a few short weeks, money was going to get really tight if something didn't give.

In the midst of her worry, an idea sprang to mind. One that involved a certain former playboy accountant, who'd wooed Channel 10's Miss Jensen not long ago. Once Stephanie Fitzpatrick arrived on the scene, it'd killed that fling before it'd even started. But that didn't mean he'd lost that social connection…

"You still on decent terms with Amber, Miles?"

He grimaced. "Barely. Though, that interview I got her with Stephanie at our last event might have helped smooth things over a bit. Why?"

"Good. Because once we have proof that Sarah was our thief, you're going to call in a favor for me. Penance for doubting my dishwasher, among other things." Her gaze shifted to the front window, where sunshine was beginning to break through the clouds. "If it's gossip this town wants, it's gossip they're going to get."

...

You should have listened.

That was today's message awaiting him at the shop. Thankfully, it was painted big as life on the alley side this time. Unfortunately, that wasn't the only message intended to ostracize him further today. "*I harbor criminals*" had been painted on Granville Hardware's storefront, and "*We hire ex-cons*" painted on the driveway side of the Checkerberry Inn.

And Cole. Was. Pissed.

He'd stormed down to the police station, demanded to speak to whoever was in charge. When they'd listened less-than-politely and told him there wasn't much they could do, he threatened to get a lawyer. That'd made the desk sergeant sit up taller, but still no help came. By the time he'd returned to the shop, Channel 10's van was parked out front, Amber Jensen knocking on his front door.

Apparently, the CLOSED sign didn't mean much to her. Too bad, as that was the way he planned to leave it. Cole had no lessons lined up that day, or any for the rest of the week, all thanks to yesterday's fiasco. And after today? Forget it, he was done.

It wasn't giving up, he told himself as he crammed as much inventory into his car as he could manage, it was cutting his losses. Sparing those closest to him from having to endure the drama that'd swooped down this past week and swallowed him whole. His grandfather had been wrong—moving forward wasn't about facing his past, it was about erasing it. And that's exactly what he planned to do: move to a new town in another state, get his name changed, and start the hell over.

He hated to leave his grandfather, and the thought of losing Maddie bordered on devastating, but he refused to be someone who put themselves before their friends and family. He'd grown up with that kind of person and swore he'd never be her. This was his chance to prove it once and for all.

Cole just prayed Maddie would understand and one day learn to forgive him.

He headed to the bank, withdrew what little he had, and then slipped in the back stairway door at his grandfather's place to grab his few belongings. All packed, he stood in the center of the room, struggling to keep his emotions in check.

He wanted to punch something. Knock down walls and throw furniture. That, and curl into a fetal position all at the same time. Instead he rushed to the bathroom and threw up the breakfast Maddie had lovingly left for him on the counter next to Fido.

See? Even now he dishonored her. God, she deserved so much better. But was he strong enough to walk away from the only woman who'd ever seen beyond his past, who didn't seem bothered about his crumby upbringing or bleak future?

He closed his eyes and pictured her beautiful face. That peaches and cream skin he could make blush with just the right look or smile. Those curves that went on forever, her hair soft as silk. The set of her lips when there was fire in her eyes.

"Oh, Madds," he whispered, head leaning back against the vanity's pedestal. "You deserve so much more."

Chapter Nineteen

Maddie paced the Checkerberry's kitchen floors that night, making herself dizzy looking between the sauces simmering on the stove and the clock across the room. Dang it, where was he already? Cole had fallen off the radar before lunch, claiming his cell's battery was about dead and he couldn't find his charger. A piss poor excuse, but she'd taken the hint and backed off. That was before Kayla had returned with good news.

News that Cole would definitely want to hear, if he ever turned back up.

A millionth glance at the clock and Maddie felt worry snake around her chest. Five after four, and he was never late. Ever.

"He show up yet?"

She spun around to see Kayla peeking through the double-doors, excitement lighting her pretty face. "No, and I'm about ready to send out a search party."

"I'm on it."

Kayla ducked back out of view, and Maddie returned her

attention to her work. Which, admittedly, is where it should be. Too bad her heart was wrecking havoc on her concentration right now.

He is going to show, she told herself. Probably just got delayed at work or ran out of gas. Two very logical explanations out of a hundred logical reasons. But deep down, she wasn't buying it. At ten after, her gut was telling a whole other tale, one that involved her, the kitchen, and no more Cole.

"He wouldn't just leave," she whispered, desperately wanting to believe it.

A knock sounded from the kitchen's side door just as Maddie was finishing chopping greens for the salad. She bolted for the door, her elbow catching an empty metal mixing bowl. It fell to the ground as she dashed by, the resulting clang echoing through the space sure to draw diners' attentions. But she didn't care. In fact, in that moment she didn't care about anything except the man who'd finally arrived. She threw open the door and dove out into the cold October air, arms open wide—

And stopped.

"Tyson? W-what are you doing here?"

. . .

Cole headed down West Deerfield Road, trying to strengthen his resolve to leave without seeing Maddie and failing miserably. He'd longed for her all day like an addict needing a fix of comfort, of love. But she'd been at work and he'd been, well, a mess. That's what vicious mobs, looming leases, and little income did to a guy, in love with an amazing woman or not.

So he'd packed his things and slid out the back door, leaving his grandfather a note and envelope with money for this month's shop lease on the kitchen table. He'd send next month's before it was due, the note promised, though he actually had other plans. Plans that would include another local musician who'd wanted that storefront. Then maybe both Granvilles could wash their hands of the place.

It sucked, watching his dreams go up in smoke and his first real relationship coming to an end before it technically got started. Him walking away from the only real family he had left. But it was the right thing to do, he told himself as the inn's drive came into view. For everyone involved.

He slowed to make the turn, glanced up the drive for any oncoming traffic, and drew to a stop. There were two people standing just outside the kitchen's side door, and even from this distance he knew by their shapes exactly who they were. Tyson stood before Maddie, a bouquet of flowers in his hands. He extended his arm toward her, and she took the flowers, bringing them to her face, then lowering them before her.

Cole's gaze slid to the envelope atop the pile of his possessions on the passenger seat. He'd meant to leave it on her windshield, his final surprise for her. This one, he knew, wouldn't bring a smile to her face like the others had. The entire ride over, he'd debated going through with his plan to leave town, to leave her. But seeing Tyson here, bringing her thoughtful gifts that went beyond silly scribbles on napkins and menus, only solidified in his mind what he already knew:

He had to set her free.

Maddie deserved more, so much more than he could possibly hope to give her. Even if his studio had taken off, the income would have been modest. Nowhere near enough to support a relationship, or a family...

No, he didn't deserve to go down that line of thinking. And while the thought of never seeing her again absolutely crushed him, deep down he knew she would be fine. Over these past few weeks, she'd stopped hiding from the world, had started to be brave, adventurous. A man like Tyson would give her all she needed, and beat the tar out of anyone who threatened to take that confidence away again.

Swallowing hard, he gave the pair one last look. They had yet to move inside. Though, at this hour, he could only guess she was thanking him for the flowers but insisting she had to get back to work. And wondering where the heck Cole was.

Guilt and regret threatened to swallow him whole.

The fading sun shone off Maddie's hair, making his fingers itch to run through its long waves one last time. But that time had passed, the memory of their night together one he would never forget. Rather than pull down the drive and deposit his letter as planned, he headed back into town to make one last stop.

Did that make him a coward? Maybe so. She'd never been an easy woman to persuade, especially on topics she felt strongly about. But this was the right thing to do, he knew in his heart. Hopefully someday she'd learn to forgive him, and would find an even stronger love with a better man. A man with a future, one who could offer her the world.

Unfortunately, Cole couldn't be him. But as he slipped the envelop under her drafty, behemoth of a front door, he was able to find a glimmer of comfort knowing he had indeed been good to his word—Cole had promised to help Maddie snag Tyson, and it seemed that's exactly what was happening. After all, Granvilles were always good to their word.

He just never imagined being good to his word would mean sacrificing his own heart along the way.

...

Maddie wasn't surprised to find her windshield note-free after work. Wasn't entirely surprised to see Cole's rarely used clunker car missing from the lot behind his grandfather's shop, either. But when she shouldered her apartment door open that evening and spied a single, plain white envelope waiting for her on the floor, well, it brought her to her knees.

Because she knew this was good-bye.

She reached for it with a shaking hand and held it close, tracing her name etched in Cole's now-familiar handwriting across its smooth surface. A hint of his sandalwood cologne still clung to the paper, though the adhesive on its flap had long since dried.

How long ago had he left it? Before his shift? After?

She drew in a deep breath, memorizing his scent, picturing his smile. But stalling wouldn't bring him back, and so with tear-filled eyes she tore the envelope open and withdrew the letter inside.

Dearest Maddie,

By now you've figured out that this won't be one of my usual after work notes. I'm afraid those are done now, gone the way of the Dodo and Saber Toothed Jackrabbits. I can only hope they entertained you half as much as they cheered me writing them. And while I will miss leaving them for you more than you can know, I'm headed west, as far from this town as the cash in my pocket will take me. Because my past, as I knew deep down it would, has found and ruined my future once again. And despite my best efforts, it's also on the verge of ruining the lives of those I love as well.

I couldn't live with myself if I stayed, choosing my own selfish needs over the livelihoods of my grandfather, of Ruby, of you. And so I've spared you all the trouble of trying to make it work or wait out the storm. The storm's over now, following me toward the Great Plains. I hope to bury it there, leave it behind along with my name and all the memories of my shitty childhood that came along with it.

Will it work? I don't know. But I'm tired of trying to hide my past, or putting the burden of helping me hide from it on those closest to me.

Please don't come looking for me. Leaving you once is killing me, and to leave you a second time would surely do me in. Because I'd have to leave you again, I'm sure of it, to protect you from the trouble I fear I'll never fully escape. And you deserve far better than that.

Far better than me.

Though, that doesn't mean I won't spend the rest of my days missing you. Never in my life have I encountered anyone as selfless, determined, sassy, and beautiful as you. Our time together these past few weeks have been hands down the best of my life—wipe that look from your face, because I'm not blowing smoke. Without you, I never would have had the chance to attempt my dream studio, or the courage to leave and bother even trying to start over.

Because of you, I have hope.

Please keep an eye on my grandfather, he's even more stubborn about not asking for help when he needs it than I am. You have every right to hate me right now, but I know out of anyone, you'll understand. So I hope one day you'll grow to forgive me, and that whenever you hear a Journey song you'll think back to our times together. And if you feel moved to sing, well, just try not to sing it too loudly (the others don't appreciate your voice nearly as much as I do).

All my love,
Your Scarecrow

His sketch of a scarecrow, doodled in the corner, was what kicked her tears into overdrive.

All their fun, all their laughter, all their commiserating.

Gone.

When at last the sobbing had faded to sniffles, and the finality of his departure began to truly set in, Maddie traded the floor for her couch. She curled up in the same corner she'd slept in last night, pulling the pillow that he'd laid on close to her chest.

"But Cole," she whispered, her gaze shifting to the darkened skies outside. "Scarecrows aren't supposed to move."

Chapter Twenty

Cole slid into the booth across from Gavin at Moe's Tavern in Remus, Michigan Friday afternoon, looking left and right out of habit if nothing else. The chances of him running into anyone else he knew in a blip on the radar like this town was about one in a billion. And while he'd liked to have been farther than half an hour from Mount Pleasant by now, this was the soonest Gavin could meet with him.

Even though his grandfather would have likely found a way out of that lease on his own, Cole refused to be irresponsible and skirt his duties like Daisy Mae always had. Bailing on Maddie and the others had been brutal enough on his conscience as it was.

"So what's the deal, Granville?" asked Gavin, twirling a fork in his right hand. "I heard you were turning the town upside down while I was out west."

"Something like that," Cole grumbled, eyeing the menu sticking cockeyed out of a cluster of condiments on the table's wall side. No, he needed to conserve what money he had, at least until he got into Illinois. Maybe there he could start looking for odd jobs, help him pay for a motel room or two as he kept moving farther west. That, or find an old abandoned barn where he could throw down a sleeping bag. At this point, both options sounded a million times better than spending one more night wedged into his car.

"Ah, a modest guy." Gavin shrugged. "Whatev, it's cool. Did you know the chick behind it all?"

"Sorry?"

"That girl and her boyfriend who got busted for painting up you and your gramps's shops. Sarah something. Guess she worked at the Checkerberry before starting this fall at her grandparents' real estate company."

Sonofagun. "Let me guess. Sheridan Realty."

"That's the one. Pa said your gramps was *pissed*. Trying to vote old Bob Sheridan out of the Elks club as we speak."

"Huh." *I hope he does.*

"Yeah, it's not often we have so much drama going on in the old part of town." Gavin grinned. "Usually, that crap stays over by the casino or on campus."

Cole shook his head. "Lucky me."

"Darn right, you are. Go from town jinx to hero overnight? Not too many cats can pull that off."

"Right. Wait, hero? What are you talking about?"

"The videotapes turned in by the Mastersons. Said if you hadn't suggested adding cameras to the inn, the string of burglaries might have gone on for weeks."

"If I hadn't suggested...?"

Maddie. She must have started that rumor. Probably got help from the others, too. Damn it, he'd left them high and dry and still they went out of their way to cover for him. But why?

Didn't matter, he couldn't go back. Cole might be viewed as a hero today—a highly undeserving one at that—but once the media took a closer look at his track record they'd see what a screw-up he really was. Or, what a screw-up his rap sheet proclaimed him to be.

A waitress arrived and asked if they were ready to order, interrupting his thoughts. When Cole tried to pass, Gavin waved him off and ordered them a basket of cheesy breadsticks, then sent the waitress off with a wink and a smile.

"I know it's too early for dinner, but you can't find better breadsticks in this state than right here at Moe's. So what is it you wanted to talk to me about anyway?"

This was it, the moment he'd been waiting for since deciding to leave Mount Pleasant. If Gavin said no, life was going to get a whole lot more complicated. If he said yes, though, things would be in order without him needing to go back. Which is the way he wanted it.

So why was he breaking into a cold sweat all of a sudden?

Cole swallowed hard and gave himself a mental kick in the pants. Now was not the time to start second-guessing his plan. This had to be done if he was going to find closure with his decision to leave. A clean break. Hopefully, the more time and distance he put between Maddie and himself, the easier it would be to get her out of his head. This close to home, she was all he could think about. He took a swig of ice water to help clear his mind, then met Gavin's curious gaze.

"You still interested in the shop?"

"Ha, was hoping you'd come to your senses one of these days and agree to take on a partner. Town's not big enough for a specialty shop like that. But guitars *and* drums? Now that's got potential. Could even bring on a bass player to offer lessons, when your schedule is—"

Cole shook his head. "Whoa, hold up. Not a partnership, I want to hand it over. As in, the whole shop."

"Why? What's wrong with the place?"

"Me—I'm wrong for the place. For the whole darned town, in case you hadn't noticed."

"So you have a rap sheet?" Gavin shrugged. "How many

rockers do you know that don't?"

"I'm not a rocker, man. Not a star, not a celebrity, not even a hero." The memory of him pushing Maddie's letter under her door drifted to mind. "Far from it."

"Look, this Sarah chick? She got to you. She found your weakness, and she exposed it to the whole town. But I'm telling you, it's over. The rumor mill? It's moved on. Sure, you might get a weird look or two from the town's oldsters for a while. But hey, join the club."

Wow, the guy was good. Suave, convincing—he'd make one heck of a salesman, that's for sure. But Cole wasn't buying it. He had been there, done that one time too many. "I'm just tired of the bull. It's time for a new start somewhere else."

"She must have really done a number on you."

Cole fought not to squirm beneath Gavin's scrutinizing gaze. Raised his glass and pretended to study its irregular lines. "It's not just about Sarah, it's—"

"I mean, I always did kinda wonder if Maddie was too much for any one man to handle."

His water glass hit the table a little harder than necessary. "Excuse me?"

"Look, you don't have to explain yourself to me, man. You're afraid of commitment, I get it."

Cole shook his head. "What are you talking about?"

"Seriously?" Gavin laughed. "You're sitting here, in this dump of a bar—"

"Hey!" yelled a guy somewhere behind them.

"Sorry, Mac!—instead of back in Mount P with your arm around one of the hottest singles in town? I mean, who *does* that if it's not because they're afraid to commit?"

Cole raked a hand through his hair to keep from punching Gavin. "Don't you get it? It doesn't matter that I'm crazy about her. I can't stay, it could ruin her. This"—he motioned between Gavin and himself—"me handing the place over, me leaving town, it's all for her."

Wasn't it?

He'd left *for* her, not because of her. Because he'd wanted to protect her, to keep her reputation free from the mud being slung his way. Or was there more?

"You tell yourself that all you want, Granville, but I know scared when I see it. And you, my brother, look like a class A scaredy cat right now."

When I ought to be the scarecrow watching over Maddie, not running away from her. Cole pounded a fist to the table. He'd already lost her, had made his bed and was sleeping in it. Could he even go back? Would she let him?

You'll never know unless you try, whispered a small voice in the back of his mind.

Or he could make things a whole lot worse, and hadn't he done enough as it was? Cole cast a wary glance at Gavin.

"You sure about the hero bit, that the town won't form an angry mob if I go back?"

"Yup. Google it, if you don't believe me. Mount Pleasant's Channel 10. Amber Jensen did you right."

"Well, I'll be." Cole cursed under his breath. He'd wanted the town to give him a chance, but hadn't stuck around long enough to let it happen. "I gotta get back, man. Gotta make this right with Maddie, with my grandfather."

"Ah, now you're talkin'." Gavin leaned forward, the glint of victory in his eyes. "The two of us? We're gonna take the town by storm. Studio by day, stage by night."

It all sounded amazing, like a dream come true. But there was still one piece missing.

"No offense, man, but if I can't win Maddie back…"

"None taken. Hmm, a woman like that, it's gonna require a lot of groveling. You'll need to come crawling back on your knees, out in public, where she can't possibly tell you no."

Cole cringed. The public was the last place he wanted to

be after the past few weeks. Unless...

"You guys still looking for a new lead guitarist?"

Gavin's smile widened. "I think I like where this is going, Granville..."

Chapter Twenty-One

Maddie did better than expected the next day at work, and the day after that when Sarah was arrested for her part in the vandalism and theft. Turns out, her most recent boyfriend Alan had a darker side than the four boyfriends prior, and she'd been all too happy to go along with it in an attempt to get even with Cole and the others. Thanks to Kayla and the Checkerberry's surveillance video, the police picked Sarah and Alan up before any more damage to the town could be done. Too bad their arrests did nothing to bring Cole back, even after the exclusive interview Miles had with Amber Jensen where he put a slightly fictitious spin on the truth and credited their kitchen help with the discovery.

Cole had been made a hero and wasn't even around to see it. The bitter irony of it all only served to fuel Maddie's bad mood further. When day three after his departure brought with it the first few bars of Journey's "Faithfully," she snapped. That's when her radio took a flying leap out the kitchen's side door.

"This belong to you?" Brent asked that afternoon,

holding the mangled device from one corner with a stick as though it were road kill.

She grunted to acknowledge his presence, then turned her back on him and focused on the beef Manhattan she was making them all for dinner that night. So far, the grunting and ignoring had served her well. Either the others were too scared to rock the boat or too afraid of the tongue-lashing that threatened to follow, because they'd handled her with kid gloves ever since…yeah.

This afternoon, however, instead of hearing the double-doors swinging open and shut once more, she heard Brent drop her radio to the floor then settle his broad frame onto one of her wobbly kitchen stools.

"Dinner won't be ready for another hour, Brent, so you might as well skedaddle."

"Maddie."

She steeled herself against the tenderness in his voice. Maddie was done with tender, done with showing weakness, done with people in general. Food was safer—it didn't talk back, leave town, or rip your heart right out of your chest. She cast a warning look over her shoulder.

"And don't you go snacking this close to dinnertime, mister. I need those apple chunks for dessert."

"*Maddie.*"

She pounded both fists on the countertop, making the potatoes she'd been peeling bounce in the colander. "What?"

"Look at me."

Mad enough to spit fire, she whirled around. "Why? So I can hear whatever lecture I have coming better? Well, I don't need a lecture, Brent. I don't need to be told how my life isn't over, or how I should just move on. I made a mistake, a six foot tall, hundred-and-ninety pound mistake, and that's my cross to bear, not any of yours."

He crossed his arms and studied her for a moment. "You

finished now?"

Maddie glared at him in silence.

"Good, because I'm sick and tired of watching you stomp around in here like a little kid who had their sucker taken away."

She felt her jaw fall slack. Brent, the soft-hearted one of the bunch, was accusing her of being...a *baby*?

"You heard me. All this pot-throwing, feet-stomping, cursing under your breath—is it really making you feel any better?"

"Yes," she snapped. His brow rose and she reconsidered. "A little. But it's not fair, damn it. Everyone else gets a happy ending except me."

Her vision began to blur, and she turned from him to hide the sudden display of weakness. "You, Miles...you guys have all the luck. The looks, the genes, the family. I've got nothing. And the one time I thought that might all change, life comes along and pulls the rug right out from under me. *Again*."

A sob broke free from her stranglehold, and Maddie curled into herself, wishing he'd just get up and walk away. But when the stool screeched across the floor, it wasn't his exit that followed, but big old Brent pulling her into a gentle bear hug.

"That's where you're wrong, Madds," he said softly. "Don't you see? Cole fell for you because of who you were, not anyone you were trying to be. You're an amazing woman. Crazy smart, wickedly funny, talented as all get out."

"But he left, Brent. If I meant so much to him, why did he leave?"

His big chin came to rest atop her head. "Because sometimes the best offense is defense."

"In layman's terms, Mr. Manly. Not athletic lingo." She jabbed him a little harder than necessary in the rib cage. Not that it mattered, Brent was about as solid as they came. A few inches taller and the guy could give Tyson a run for his money.

"He left to protect you, just like his letter said."

Maddie drew back and gave him an incredulous look, but Brent just shrugged.

"What? My fiancée and I do actually speak once in a while. When we're not busy, you know, doing other th—"

"La-la-la," she said, stepping away to cover her ears. *Gotta start rationing their Key lime pie...* "Great, so he left me to protect me. But what if I didn't need protecting? Why didn't I get a say in the matter?"

Brent's right brow rose once more, and Maddie exhaled in defeat.

"Yeah, okay," she said. "So I probably wouldn't have listened."

"Look, I know it sucks right now. But you've come so far. Don't close yourself off to the world again after one whirlwind adventure that ended too soon. Heck, Tyson's still hanging around—maybe he can help ease the sting a bit."

Maddie barked a laugh. "Ha, no. Tyson's been hanging around because he's trying to convince me to come work for him during the inn's offseason. Seems his little smoothie café inside the gym caught on in a big way, and corporate wants to use their site as a test ground for an expanded menu."

"Wow, that's great. You gonna do it?"

She shrugged. "Probably. Don't have much of anything else to do."

The thought of sitting around her apartment, bored and missing Cole, made her cringe. Besides, it'd be kinda nice not to have to worry so much about money during the colder months. A grin stretched across Brent's face.

"What's that look for?"

"Oh, nothing," he said, reaching to retrieve his items from the floor.

"Nothing my rear. What are you up to, Masterson?"

"Guess you'll have to come to the gala on Saturday to find out."

The gala—she'd nearly forgotten about it. Images of Cole, teasing her about asking Tyson to the stupid event threatened to surface. She gave them a mental shove aside and mumbled, "I'm not going."

"Your loss," he said with a wink, heading for the door. "Though, I strongly recommend you reconsider."

With that he was gone, leaving her to consider all he'd said. As much as she hated to admit it, he was right on all counts. Cole hadn't left to hurt her, he'd done the only thing he knew how in an attempt to spare her from the same pain and humiliation he'd experienced. Still didn't make it any easier. And yet, she didn't hate him like she expected to. Or the entire male population, surprisingly.

Didn't mean she was ready to go on the prowl for another man anytime soon, though. But the thought of crawling under another rock for the next seven years didn't appeal to her, either. Maddie considered Brent's reminder about the gala, the taunt that it was, as she turned back to her half-peeled potatoes.

"Maybe," she whispered to the spuds. "But don't count on it."

Chapter Twenty-Two

Maddie made her way into Mount Pleasant's country club, checked her coat at the registration table with a gal whose lipstick was far too pink for anyone with half a grain of dignity to wear, and angled for the main room. All of Stephanie's planning had paid off—the place looked amazing. Brightly colored balloons were tethered in clusters around the room, each with the FITS logo. Banners displaying happy children running across soccer fields and tennis courts adorned every wall, save for the far one which was blocked by a makeshift stage and the musical instruments set upon it in waiting.

"Maddie! Over here!"

She turned to spy Brent and Kayla seated with Ruby and Old Tom. The youngsters and the oldsters, all paired up and happy, happy, happy. Yay.

No, Maddie told herself as she crossed the room—slowly, so she didn't kill herself in the high heels Steph and Kayla had picked out for her—she was not going to be that way. This event was to support underprivileged kids, downers need not apply. Besides, Brent had hinted at an announcement of some sort. If she were placing bets, it was that Miles was going to pop the question tonight to Stephanie. Then again, neither of them seemed in as big a hurry to tie the knot as Brent and Kayla.

"Hey, guys. Did I miss anything?" she asked, lowering into an open seat beside Ruby.

"Nope," said Kayla. "Just Miles making his *big* announcement."

"Aw, man. Seriously? That's the whole reason I came!"

Brent gave her a wary look. "To hear him rattle off the menu selections?"

"Wait, what?" She looked to Kayla, who burst out laughing.

"Sorry, I can't help it," Kayla said. "He was so nervous about it, paced the hall all afternoon while doing voice warm ups."

"Man, he can be such a girl sometimes," said Maddie.

Brent reached over and gave her a fist bump.

"Oh, you two just stop it." Ruby swatted at them both. "Miles did a wonderful job. And doesn't Stephanie look radiant tonight?"

They all looked to Steph, who did indeed look amazing as ever. Tonight, she was in a deep burgundy gown, tight on top, long and flowy on the bottom. Maddie sighed. Oh, to have a figure like that.

"So, when is the *real* big announcement coming?" she asked, reaching for the nearest untouched glass of ice water.

"Soon, I think."

Maddie looked up in time to see Brent and Kayla exchange a knowing grin.

"Please tell me you two aren't up to something."

"No, they aren't," said Ruby, patting her hand. "Though, do make sure you see Miles before the night is over, dear. I believe he has someone from the board he'd like you to meet."

Maddie withdrew her hand, trying to keep her smile polite. Already? Cole had been gone just over a week and the Mastersons were already scoping out her next target? Well, that was just too darned bad. Yes, Brent had helped get her out of her mental rut, but that didn't mean she was gunning to get back on the dating bandwagon. Not yet; her heart needed time to heal.

"Thanks, Ruby, but I'm sure I'm not interested."

. . .

"Is she out there?" Cole asked as Gavin reentered the back hall.

"Just walked in." He winked at Cole. "And looks absolutely stunning. Great call on the deep blue dress."

"Thank you, Kayla," he mumbled.

His gratitude toward her extended far beyond helping Maddie select the perfect dress, of course. She and Brent had helped plant the seeds to get Maddie here, to the gala. Kayla had also spent a few days last week working up a website for him and Gavin's new shop, M 'n' G Music. Already they'd had dozens of calls, and their lesson slots were slowly filling up.

The dream business was becoming a reality. Now it was time to get the girl and, hopefully, live happily ever after.

"You ready, lover boy?" asked Miles, walking in to give Cole a hearty clap on the back.

"Ready as I'll ever be. But remember—you promised to stay close to her table. If she goes for the dinner knives, call 911."

Miles laughed. "Will do. Of course, it'll be from my cell phone, down the street. I've seen Maddie's aim, buddy. She doesn't miss, especially with knives."

He pushed through a door and disappeared back into the main room.

"Your girl part carnie, Granville, or what?"

Cole grinned at Gavin, shaking his head. "Nah, but lethal all the same. And I wouldn't ask her to change a thing."

"Then let's do this. Come on, boys."

The members of Radar Love made their way through the same door Miles had stepped through a moment ago, and arrived to hear him announce the band. Polite applause followed, and Gavin chuckled.

"Sounds like we've got our work cut out for us."

Cole held back, letting his other bandmates step around the stage's rear black curtain. He picked up his guitar, flicked the wireless amp on, slid his earpiece into place, then looked to the ceiling and whispered, "Could use a little help tonight, Pops. This one's a bit higher than what I'm used to covering."

On the other side of the curtain, Gavin was getting the crowd warmed up. Cheers sounded, more applause. "And this first one is going out to a special someone."

The lights dimmed, and someone in the crowd hooted. Gavin chuckled. "That's right, she'll know who she is."

That was his cue. Cole took a deep breath, counted off for the keyboardist, then started in with the guitar lick from Journey's "Lights."

He stepped from around the curtain, squinting past the canned lights pointed at the stage. It only took a moment to spot her, sitting beside Ruby and his grandfather, both of whose white-haired heads nearly glowed in the dimmed lighting. Her mouth was drawn into a surprised *O*, and—thank the good lord—no cutlery was in her grip.

She raised a hand to her mouth, shaking her head and exchanging words with Kayla. And though he didn't have a clue what was being said, he didn't care. All that mattered was she hadn't walked out, which meant he still had a chance.

Cole did the best he could to cover the tune, hitting the high notes and nailing the guitar riffs, all while singing about missing his girl while on the road. And everything he did on stage—the notes, the lyrics, the pleading his case—he directed to Maddie. He sang his heart out, and the song ended to an eruption of applause.

But applause wasn't what he wanted. Maddie was.

Cole set his guitar down, hopped from the stage, and headed toward her table. Gavin and the boys kicked into another song, allowing him time to make things right. She rose from her seat and…proceeded toward the exit.

Of course she wasn't going to make this easy. It was Maddie, after all.

He burst through the doors a second after her, but found himself alone in the lobby. Cole raked a hand through his hair, trying to keep calm. She couldn't have gone far, not in those heels.

"So. You're back."

He spun to the right, and realized he wasn't alone after all. A large ficus had concealed Maddie from his initial glance. He moved tortoise slow in her direction, praying she would stay put and hear him out.

"For you."

"Uh-huh." Maddie paused. "A phone call would have been nice. Maybe a hug good-bye."

Okay, she was talking. That was a good sign, right?

"Phone died. And you were busy with Tyson when I came to deliver…"

"Your letter?" She stepped forward, red-rimmed eyes narrowed. "Probably best for all of us I didn't find that on my windshield."

He knew he'd hurt her, but seeing her this way made him feel that much worse. She'd been happy, so happy. And then he'd gotten all stupid and stolen that happiness away.

Never again.

"I was afraid." He came to stand before her.

"Smart man."

"And an idiot."

She smirked. "Getting warmer."

He took her hands in his. "And if you can ever learn to forgive me, I promise to never leave you again."

"Never?"

The fury faded from her eyes, replaced by a wary hopefulness. Cole pulled her into his arms and pressed a kiss to the top of her head.

"Wouldn't be much of a scarecrow if I kept wandering off, now would I?"

Maddie laughed softly. "Don't even think you're out of the doghouse just yet, buddy. There's gonna be a whole lot more groveling ahead from you than this. And making up back in my apartment."

"I'll grovel the rest of the day if it'll lead me back to your place tonight."

A door behind them swished opened and both turned to see who it was.

"Uh, Cole?" said Miles. "They need you back up on stage."

"Yeah, I'll be right there." He looked back to Maddie as Miles disappeared from view. "That is, if you don't mind."

She chuckled. "Go, Mr. Celebrity. Your public awaits."

"You sure? I mean, I just got back. The guys could do a few more without me if—"

Maddie tugged his shirt and pulled his face before hers. "Cole? Just kiss me already so you can get back to the band."

So demanding, so understanding, so…Maddie.

Cole tipped her chin toward his and whispered, "Yes, ma'am."

Epilogue

Maddie bent to pull a pan of cornbread stuffing from the oven as the kitchen doors *swooshed* open and closed behind her.

"Don't even think about it, Masterson," she said with her back to the intruder.

"Dang it, Maddie," said Miles. "When exactly did you grow those eyes in the back of your head?"

"When I started working with you and your thieving cousin. Now drop the turkey leg, and no one gets hurt."

More grumbling sounded behind her, followed by someone sucking their fingers clean. She set the cornbread down and shot him a dark look.

"What?" he said, hands in the air. "I dropped it like you said. See?"

"Why aren't you in the dining room with the others?"

"Because they're all starving and wanted someone to come in and see what was taking so long. I drew the short straw."

Maddie grinned. "Well, you're in luck, that was the last of it. If you can get a few helpers, we'll have dinner on the table in no time."

"Perfect. Then you won't be needing this." He grabbed the drumstick and sprinted back out the doors.

"Miles David Masterson!" exclaimed Ruby from the other room. "You put that turkey leg down this minute!"

Maddie shook her head and crossed the kitchen to grab a serving bowl for the stuffing. Brent and Cole appeared to help transport the last of the meal to the table, Cole hanging back long enough to press a soft kiss to her cheek.

"It smells like heaven in here."

"It better." She laughed. "This is the toughest meal I'm asked to make all year."

"What are you talking about? You've made dozens of dishes more complex than this."

"Yes, but expectations are higher for this meal than any other. If the bird's too dry or stuffing too moist, I'll never live it down."

"Well, then I guess it's good I'm coming to the table without any expectations," he said with a wink. "My Thanksgivings growing up looked a lot more like the Peanuts version."

"Let me guess—you were in charge of the toast."

"Texas toast, to be exact."

"Of course." She pecked a kiss on his cheek and gave his butt a bump with her own. "We'd better get on out there, or toast is all we'll have left."

"Good point."

They joined the others and took the two open seats between Stephanie and Kayla.

Two, not one. Maddie couldn't help but grin.

The past few weeks had gone by in a blink, with business at the inn winding down and business at Cole's shop—now run in conjunction with his buddy Gavin—kicking into gear. Truthfully, the timing couldn't have been any better. And much to everyone's relief, between Gavin's connections and the spotlight Amber Jensen aired on their new shop, Mount Pleasant seemed to have accepted Cole as one of their own.

Finally, everything seemed to be falling into place for him. And Maddie couldn't be happier for Cole. Of course, when he was happy, she was happy, and their future together was definitely looking bright.

"Thomas," said Ruby. "Would you do us the honor and say grace?"

"Certainly. Our Heavenly Father…"

Maddie tried to listen, but when Old Tom began to ramble her thoughts drifted to the past year at the inn and all the blessings that'd come with it. To Brent taking over as groundskeeper, and Kayla arriving pre-season, stranded in an ice storm and then staying on as their marketing guru/assistant innkeeper. To Miles's near departure, and the arrival of Stephanie, who'd finally managed to tame the playboy and cure him of his wanderlust. To Cole, who had joined them part-time this fall in the kitchen, his heart of gold capturing her own. As Tom said "Amen," she sat beside his grandson thinking life couldn't get much better.

The meal, thank goodness, proved to be one of her best. Everything had come out just right, even the scalloped corn that she sometimes fought with. Compliments abounded, and soon the group was full, lethargic, and patting full bellies with smiles on their faces.

No sight pleased a chef more.

Relieved that the meal had gone off without a hitch, Maddie rose to begin clearing plates. "Anyone want dessert?"

A collective groan rose from the table.

"Actually, Madds, have a seat," said Brent. "There's something Kayla and I want to share."

All eyes shifted to Kayla as her cheeks took on a rosy hue.

"I know we'd originally set our wedding date for next

June," he said, "but she's asking that we move it up to January. Something about not wanting to outgrow her dress…"

Stephanie let out a shriek and sprang from her chair to embrace Kayla. "I knew it! I knew when you passed up the wine last weekend that something was up."

"Well, both our clocks are starting to tick," she said with a shrug and radiant smile. "So we figured we'd just let nature take its course."

Miles met Maddie's gaze in the midst of the continuing congratulations. She pointed to the happy couple and mouthed the words "*Key lime pie.*"

He just laughed, then looked to Stephanie's empty plate and back, his eyes wide and smile slipping. "Need to cut back," he answered in a loud whisper.

Maddie winked. Miles could say that all he wanted, but she knew Stephanie had a plan of her own. Besides, now that Kayla was pregnant, baby fever was sure to descend on the Checkerberry Inn. Perhaps it was a good thing it was now officially closed for the season. Otherwise, things might look a whole lot different by this time next year.

Ruby shushed everyone, then cleared her throat. "Brent, Kayla, we are all so very happy for you. And how exciting it is, as we look forward to welcoming the next generation of Mastersons into the inn." She looked to Tom, who gave her a wink. "I wanted to let you all know that Thomas and I have some exciting news as well."

The room fell instantly silent, save for Stephanie who giggled at the look of concern on Miles's face.

"I'm pretty sure your grandmother isn't expecting, too, darling," she whispered.

"No, dear," said Ruby. "But changes are indeed coming. First, with my name."

Old Tom rose from his seat and placed both hands upon Ruby's shoulders. "I hope you all don't mind my not asking your permission first, but I've asked your grandmother for her hand in marriage."

"About darned time," muttered Brent under his breath with a grin.

A fresh round of congratulations was exchanged, ending with Kayla dabbing her eyes.

"Sorry," she mumbled. "Silly hormones kicking in already."

"So we get the name change, Grandma," said Miles. "What other surprise are you planning to spring on us tonight?"

"We're eloping over Christmas." Ruby's smile widened. "And becoming snow birds. Don't worry, though. We'll come back for your January wedding."

The room fell instantly silent, cousins and staff exchanging confused looks.

"But Ruby," asked Miles. "How will you prep the inn for next season from down there?"

"I won't," she said, her smile unwavering. "I think it's high time to listen to your advice, boys, and retire."

"Retire?" Maddie said, breaking her silence. "Are you selling the inn?"

"Heavens no," said Ruby. "Merely handing it over to my grandsons. Seeing as I've taught them all I know, the Checkerberry will do just fine."

"And the hardware store?" Cole asked.

Old Tom smiled. "Don't worry about my store, son, you focus on your music. I'll have my hands in the operations for several years to come, even if it's across phone lines a few months of the year."

"Phone lines?" Kayla shook her head. "We're gonna need to set you two up with laptops, and iPads, and Skype, and..."

Maddie felt Cole's hand rest upon her knee beneath the table. She turned to meet his gaze, concern clear in his eyes.

"You okay?" she whispered.

"Yeah, just nervous to think of Ruby and my grandfather being so far away," he said. "What if something happens?"

"First, this is Ruby and Old Tom we're talking about. Both tough as nails. And second, they said snow birds, which means they'll be back here half the year."

"Yeah, I guess so."

She looked around the table at all the smiling faces, so near and dear to her heart. They'd hired her at the inn, made her one of their own, and forever changed her life. And, crazy as it could be at times, Maddie wouldn't want it any other way.

She rested her hand atop his and gave it a little squeeze.

"Besides, I think between all of us, they'll have more than enough reason to come back and visit the Checkerberry for many years to come."

Acknowledgments

This series would not have been possible without all of my amazing family, friends, and fans who supported me during its development. The Checkerberry Inn has become a second home to me, its characters near and dear to my heart. Special thanks goes to my editor, Alycia, for helping me bring the characters and their stories to life, to the wonderful staff at Bliss, and to Entangled Publishing for believing in me and my stories.

About the Author

Kyra Jacobs is an extroverted introvert who writes of love, humor, and mystery in the Midwest and beyond. Her romance novels range from sweet contemporaries to romantic suspense and paranormal/fantasy. No matter the setting, Kyra employs both comedy and chaos to help her characters find inspiration and/or redemption on their way to happily ever after.

When the Hoosier native isn't pounding out scenes for her next book, she's likely outside, elbow-deep in snapdragons or spending quality time with her sports-loving family. Kyra also loves to read, tries to golf, and is an avid college football fan.

Be sure to stop by her website www.KyraJacobs.wordpress.com to learn more about her novels and ways to connect with her on social media.

Discover the **Checkerberry Inn** *series…*

HER UNEXPECTED DETOUR

HER UNEXPECTED ENGAGEMENT

Find your Bliss with these great releases...

HER COWBOY'S PROMISE
a *Fly Creek* novel by Jennifer Hoopes

Artist Emily White's grief sent her to the small town of Fly Creek. Since then, she's kept her emotions safely tucked away—until she meets the new rancher at Sky Lake Dude Ranch. Adam Conley is only in town for as long as it takes to fulfill his promise to his late cousin. The last thing he expects is the instant attraction to the reason he's in town. Emily is beautiful, vibrant, and completely off-limits.

HATE TO LOVE HIM
a *Kendrick Place* novel by Jody Holford

Whenever Brady Davis and Mia Kendrick are in the same room, sparks fly—both the bad and good kind. Brady's worried Mia's focus on big business could be the end of the tight-knit community he's created at Kendrick Place, while Mia can't ever let another man stand in the way of her dreams. Brady could have the power to change her mind...if he can get inside her heart.

DATING THE WRONG MR. RIGHT
a *Sisters of Wishing Bridge* novel by Amanda Ashby

Ben Cooper is doing his best to build his business and help his parents. The last thing he needs is the distraction that is Pepper Watson. She's prickly every time he's in her presence, but he sees another side of her. And kissing her is pretty much the best thing that's ever happened to him. He's putting down roots. She's running away. It's going to take more than a wish for these two to find their happily ever after.

THE DOCTOR'S REDEMPTION
a *Shadow Creek, Montana* novel by Victoria James

Gwen Bailey has been taking care of everyone but herself. After a tragedy tore her family apart, she put her dreams aside. Now that her life is on track, she can concentrate on snagging the mysterious customer who has her dreaming about her own happy ending, but it's only a matter of time before the truth comes out and Dr. Luke Thomson knows Gwen won't forgive him once she discovers his secret…